MW01292461

THE
NARNIA
COOKBOOK

The World of NARNIA™

THE
NARNIA
COOKBOOK

FOODS FROM C. S. LEWIS'S

The Chronicles of Narnia

COMMENTARY BY DOUGLAS GRESHAM
ILLUSTRATIONS BY PAULINE BAYNES

HarperCollinsPublishers

*The publisher gratefully acknowledges the help and support of
Elizabeth Stevens at Curtis Brown Ltd. Her invaluable assistance
and advice is greatly appreciated. The publisher would also
like to thank Mary Kate Morgan for her research and culinary
expertise in the preparation of these recipes.*

Quotations throughout the book are taken from *The Chronicles of Narnia*®, written by C. S. Lewis:

THE MAGICIAN'S NEPHEW
THE LION, THE WITCH AND THE WARDROBE
THE HORSE AND HIS BOY
PRINCE CASPIAN
THE VOYAGE OF THE *DAWN TREADER*
THE SILVER CHAIR
THE LAST BATTLE

These quotations are used with the permission of C.S. Lewis Pte. Ltd.
"Narnia," "The World of Narnia," and "The Lion, the Witch and the Wardrobe" are trademarks of C.S. Lewis Pte. Ltd.
"The Chronicles of Narnia" is a U.S. Registered Trademark of C.S. Lewis Pte. Ltd.

The Narnia Cookbook: Foods from C. S. Lewis's The Chronicles of Narnia
Commentary copyright © 1998 by Douglas Gresham
Recipe collection copyright © 1998 by HarperCollins Publishers
Illustrations copyright © 1998 by HarperCollins Publishers
All rights reserved. No part of this book may be used or reproduced in any manner whatsoever without written permission except in the case of brief quotations embodied in critical articles and reviews. Printed in the United States of America. For information address HarperCollins Children's Books, a division of HarperCollins Publishers, 10 East 53rd Street, New York, NY 10022.   http://www.harperchildrens.com

Library of Congress Cataloging-in-Publication Data
Gresham, Douglas H., 1945–
  The Narnia cookbook : foods from C. S. Lewis's the Chronicles of Narnia / commentary by Douglas Gresham ; illustrations by Pauline Baynes.
      p.   cm.
  Summary: A collection of recipes devised from some of the foods mentioned in the Chronicles of Narnia, along with a history of the dishes and anecdotes from Lewis's life.
  ISBN 0-06-027815-3
  1. Cookery — Juvenile literature. 2. Lewis, C. S. (Clive Staples), 1898–1963. Chronicles of Narnia — Juvenile literature.
[1. Cookery. 2. Lewis, C. S. (Clive Staples), 1898–1963. Chronicles of Narnia.] I. Baynes, Pauline, ill. II. Lewis, C. S. (Clive Staples), 1898–1963. Chronicles of Narnia. III. Title.
TX652.5.G728   1998
641.5—DC21   98–10657
                                                                                                                  CIP
                                                                                                                   AC

Typography by Tom Starace and David Horowitz
1   2   3   4   5   6   7   8   9   10
❖
First Edition

CONTENTS

◆

A WORD ABOUT SAFETY

When you work in the kitchen, it is important to be very careful not to cut or burn yourself. You may need the help of an adult to prepare many of the foods in this book, especially if you are going to use a sharp knife and electrical appliances, and work with a hot stove or oven. Be sure an adult is present with you at all times when you are in the kitchen, ready to cook these wonderful recipes. By following some simple rules, you will be able to work safely and have fun!

- If you have long hair, tie it back, and roll up long sleeves carefully.
- Ask an adult for help when using sharp knives or shears and appliances such as electric mixers, blenders, can openers, etc.
- Pick up knives by the handle, never by the blade.
- Always have an adult handle hot or boiling liquids. Do not fry foods yourself.
- Use heavy pot holders for handling hot pots and pans on the stove and baking dishes from the oven.
- Never leave the stove unattended.
- Be sure to ask an adult to light an oven for you, if it is not self-starting.
- Do not ever light matches yourself!
- Be sure to turn off electric appliances such as mixers or blenders before taking the lids off.
- Never place any electrical item in water.

- Use a plastic cutting board to cut up raw poultry, meat, or fish. Wash the board with hot soapy water after every use and before using it with another type of food.

- Never put cooked poultry, fish, or meat on the same board or in the same container that held the raw meat, unless you have washed the container well first.

- Don't use cracked or dirty eggs. They may have been contaminated with harmful bacteria. Be sure to wash your hands, the equipment, and the countertop after working with eggs. Avoid eating raw eggs.

- Keep hot foods hot. Raw eggs, fish, poultry, and meat must be cooked well to kill harmful bacteria. If you have leftovers, put them into covered containers and refrigerate or freeze them as soon as possible.

- Keep cold foods cold. Foods that are meant to be refrigerated should be cold when you touch them. Frozen foods should be extremely cold and hard as a rock. Thaw foods in the refrigerator, not on the countertop.

FOREWORD

This cookbook is about more than just cooking or food. It's about Narnia and Jack (C. S. Lewis), the man who wrote *The Chronicles of Narnia*, and food and you and me. But mostly it's about Narnia, food, and fun. Jack was born in Belfast, Ireland, in 1898. When Jack was a boy, Belfast was an unhealthy place to live and his parents were very careful about not letting him and his older brother, Warnie, get cold and wet, so the boys spent a lot of time indoors. As a result, Jack became quite interested in what went on in the kitchen. Jack's mother, Flora, used a book already famous in those days called *The Book of Household Management*, by Mrs. Isabella Beeton, that contained several thousand recipes; and many of Jack's favorite dishes originally came from this book. Many years later it was Jack himself who showed me how to cook things like grilled kippers (smoked herring), which he had learned from watching the cook in Belfast all those years before.

Many of the foods Jack preferred might be considered old-fashioned in today's world. In the days of his youth, many of the ingredients available were fresher than those available today. There were no supermarkets or freezers or even refrigerators, and things like meat, dairy products, fish, and bread were brought to the house each day by the butchers, milkmen, fishmongers, and bakers (although many people made their own bread at home). Vegetables were often grown at home in kitchen gardens just as they are in Narnia, or if you lived in a town, they were often delivered by a greengrocer. Old-fashioned foods like those preferred in Narnia are some of the very best-tasting foods, and quite often the most nutritious as well. Remember that in those days, as in Narnia to this day, there were no prepackaged foods or processed foods, no chemicals were added, and no artificial fertilizers or pesticides were used in growing foods. Fruit and vegetables might not have looked as beautiful as they do today, but they tasted better. If you have been to Narnia or if you grow your own vegetables at home, or if you have relatives or friends who have their own gardens, you will know the difference in taste between those and the ones from the supermarket. Free-range eggs are another example. They are rich-tasting, richly colored eggs, which are always better than those produced in factory farms.

Back in Jack's day and also in Narnia, profit was not as important as people think it to be here in this world. Pride in one's work or products played a much higher role in the way people did things. For example, a man who sold bacon and ham in those days would go to a great deal of trouble to ensure that his products were the very best they could possibly be. He would mix up his own special recipe of "pickling brine," a mixture of salt, water, sometimes molasses and sugar, a little saltpeter, and his own secret herbs and spices. It was very important to get the brine absolutely right. He would then cure the bacon in the brine for ten days or so (depending on the weather), and then smoke it in his own smokehouse, having carefully chosen the best wood for his smoke-fire. In England or Ireland, this would be good dry oak; in America it would be hickory. In Narnia the dwarfs make the most delicious bacon. People everywhere went to immense trouble and took great pride in their products.

Jack liked good food and good company. He enjoyed nothing more than a fine dinner in the company of people whom he liked and respected and with whom he could enjoy good conversation. As a fellow of a college at Oxford, Jack was greatly privileged to be able to dine "in hall" at the college. There he would partake of the excellent cooking that the college provided, while surrounded by academics and learned men, many of whom were great conversationalists.

At his home in Oxford, for many years Jack ate very simple foods. But when he married my mother late in his life, soon his meals rivaled any of his old college's. My mother was such an excellent cook, her meals might have been fine enough to grace the tables at Cair Paravel.

It's often said that you are what you eat, which perhaps is a bit of a stretch of the imagination. But it is true that you can find out quite a lot about people by observing what they eat. Now, in Narnia—that wonderful, magical place—the foods mentioned are mostly things that Jack himself liked to eat. Of course there are exceptions, like Man Pies and Marsh-wiggle and other things eaten by the evil giants and other nasties, which perhaps it is better not to go into. On the whole, though, Narnian food is utterly delightful.

What we have done in this book is to take a number of the foods mentioned in *The Chronicles of Narnia* and then devise recipes for preparing them.

As you go through this book and try the recipes, remember that in Narnia there are no electrical appliances, and we have tried to keep the use of blenders and other modern appliances to a minimum. We have also had to substitute for a few things here and there that simply don't exist in our world. Pavenders, for example, are a beautiful salt and freshwater fish found in the rivers and seas of Narnia but not here. We have used salmon instead, which is the most similar fish this world has to offer.

As you cook these recipes, please be very careful to treat the food and the utensils with the respect they deserve, and to watch out for hot things and sharp things. It's no fun cooking if you or somebody else gets hurt. Have fun and eat hearty.

—Douglas Gresham

BREAKFAST

Breakfast is a word that means "to start eating again after a time spent not eating anything"—to break one's fast. Different countries have different breakfast traditions. In France breakfast is usually a cup of coffee with a pastry and perhaps a piece of fruit. In Australia and America, steak and eggs are not uncommon for breakfast. In Ireland or England, as well as in Narnia, a wide variety of foods are preferred for breakfast. Porridge, for example, is a common breakfast food. Grilled kippers, fried bacon, eggs, sausages, black and white puddings, kidneys, and mushrooms have been popular down through the ages. Of course, we have to remember that in Narnia there are many different kinds of animals and creatures, and they all have their own tastes and preferences. While Dwarfs would prepare a typical fried breakfast, Pattertwig the squirrel would serve a selection of the lighter nuts. The breakfasts we have in this book are those Narnian breakfasts that are suitable for Sons of Adam and Daughters of Eve.

PORRIDGE

Porridge originates in Scotland, where the climate is such that oats grow well. The first porridge was probably made of oats, winnowed to remove most of the husks, and then bashed with a rock and boiled in water. In Britain you can still get old-fashioned stone-ground porridge, just as in the old days when grains were ground between big flat stones in wind- or water-powered mills. To this day, in parts of Scotland and Narnia, porridge is eaten with salt, as a savory food. Many of the people of northern Ireland originally came from Scotland, and Jack sometimes liked his porridge with salt and sometimes sweet. In Narnia quite a few of the creatures like porridge—Giants, Dwarfs, Fauns, Centaurs, and others—and because sugar is imported from Calormen, and there is honey in Narnia and salt from the sea, they eat their porridge either way.

"And here's porridge—and here's a jug of cream—and here's a spoon."
—THE HORSE AND HIS BOY

4 SERVINGS

2 cups milk
1½ cups water
¼ teaspoon salt
2 cups rolled oats, 5-
   minute style

4 SERVINGS

4 cups water
¼ teaspoon salt
1 scant cup steel-cut
   oats

Quick Porridge

1. In a medium saucepan, bring the milk, water, and salt to a boil.

2. Stir in the oats and return to the boil.

3. Lower heat and cook slowly for about 5 minutes, stirring occasionally.

Old-fashioned Porridge

1. In a medium saucepan, bring the water and salt to a boil.

2. Stir in the oats and return to the boil, continuing to stir for a minute or so.

3. Lower heat and simmer until the oats are tender and the water is absorbed, adding more water if necessary, about 20-30 minutes.

◆ Either version of porridge should be served hot with milk or cream and honey and, if you like, a sprinkle of salt. For a delicious change in flavor try a spoonful of brown sugar or cane syrup.

BACON, EGGS, AND MUSHROOMS

One of the most delicious smells in the entire world is the smell of smoked bacon frying in a pan on a frosty morning. You can get hungry just thinking about it. Put in some fresh free-range eggs and it gets even better. Add some English button mushrooms, and you have a feast almost too good to eat only at breakfast time. Bacon, eggs, and mushrooms with fresh bread and butter and a glass of fresh milk is one of my very favorite meals. Jack liked mushrooms probably more than anything else, and he loved this particular recipe. In Narnia the Dwarfs are wonderful cooks, and this meal is one their most favorite dishes.

"It was, in fact, the smell of bacon and eggs and mushrooms all frying in a pan."
—THE HORSE AND HIS BOY

1. In a nonstick frying pan over medium heat, cook the bacon, turning now and then, until firm but not crispy. Add the mushrooms and cook until they are wilted. Push the bacon and mushrooms to one side of the pan, and tilt the pan so the fat runs down to the other side. Crack the eggs into a saucer and slide them into the fat, keeping the pan tilted until the eggs are set. When they are firm enough to stay in place, set the pan flat on the stove, cover, and cook until the eggs are done.

2. Drain off the excess fat and place on a warmed plate. Serve with the toast.

PER PERSON:

2 pieces thick sliced bacon
2 white button mushrooms, cleaned, stems trimmed even with base of cap
2 large eggs
2 slices bread, toasted, lightly buttered, and halved diagonally

Scrambled Eggs and Toast (Mumbled Eggs)

For a light meal, you can't beat scrambled eggs. What we have here is the basic scrambled eggs recipe that has been used for ages and ages all over Narnia. If you want to get adventurous, you can add a few different herbs and spices. But be careful—too much garlic or too much chili could ruin the flavor. Faun Orruns would probably toss in a few finely chopped chives or a touch of garlic because Fauns have delicate and well-refined tastes, though they are light eaters. One interesting thing about scrambled eggs is that you can eat a lot more eggs when they are scrambled than you can if they are fried or boiled.

Breakfast was scrambled eggs and toast and
Eustace tackled it just as if he had not
had a very large supper in the middle of the night.
—*The Silver Chair*

Per person:

2 slices firm white or
  wheat bread, toasted,
  lightly buttered, and
  halved diagonally
2 tablespoons butter
2 large eggs
Salt and pepper to taste

1. Keep the toast warm while preparing the eggs.

2. Warm a nonstick pan and melt the butter over low heat. Break the eggs into the pan and cook over medium heat, stirring in one direction until the mixture begins to set.

3. With a wooden spoon, pull the egg mixture away from the sides of the pan, and stir the eggs just enough to keep from sticking to the pan.

4. When the eggs are cooked but still soft, sprinkle with a little salt and pepper and turn out onto warm plates. Tuck a triangle of toast on each side of the eggs and serve while piping hot.

BUTTERED EGGS

It was not such a breakfast as they would have chosen, for Caspian and Cornelius were thinking of venison pasties, and Peter and Edmund of buttered eggs and hot coffee.

—PRINCE CASPIAN

1. Keep the toast warm while preparing the eggs. Warm the serving plates.

2. Break the eggs into a large bowl, season lightly with salt and pepper, and beat with a fork until well mixed.

3. Put the butter into a warmed nonstick pan to melt. Do not let it get too hot. When it is melted, pour in the eggs and cook over low heat. Stir the eggs constantly in the same direction, breaking up any lumps that form.

4. When the eggs are thick and creamy, remove the pan from the heat and continue stirring the eggs for a minute. Arrange 2 pieces of toast on each plate and top with the buttered eggs. Garnish with parsley and serve.

6 SERVINGS

6 slices firm white or
   wheat bread, toasted,
   lightly buttered, and
   halved diagonally
12 large eggs
Salt and pepper
12 tablespoons butter (1½
   sticks)
Sprigs of parsley

EVERYDAY WHITE BREAD

Almost every country in the world has some form of bread. When Jack was a child, bread was made in the home. There are two kinds of bread that Jack loved: yeast bread (as in this recipe) and Irish soda bread, which is made without yeast. Making bread at home is good fun and, when you get it right, provides you with beautiful, fresh, rich-tasting loaves. It is also very healthy because, like Narnia bread, it has no chemical additives. When making bread, it is best to keep your ingredients, implements, and working surfaces warm. You should also remember that for best results you must knead the bread firmly. The only problem with homemade bread is that people eat it as fast as you can pull it from the oven. In Narnia, it is the Dwarfs and Fauns who are the best bread makers.

> *Meanwhile the girls were helping Mrs. Beaver to fill the kettle and lay the table and cut the bread.*
> —THE LION, THE WITCH AND THE WARDROBE

3 LOAVES

5 cups unbleached all-
   purpose flour, plus more
   if needed
1 tablespoon salt
6 tablespoons (3/4 stick)
   butter, room tempera-
   ture
1 packet or 1 tablespoon
   active dry yeast
1 teaspoon granulated
   sugar
1 cup lukewarm water
   (110–115 degrees F)
1 cup lukewarm milk

1. In the bowl of a heavy-duty mixer, combine 5 cups of the flour and the salt. Cut the butter into small pieces and rub into the flour with your fingers until well combined.

2. In a cup or small bowl, stir the yeast and sugar into the water until they dissolve. Let stand for 5 minutes until the mixture is creamy in appearance and forms small bubbles on top. This is called proofing and shows that the yeast is active.

3. Use a dough hook on the mixer,* and set the mixer at the lowest speed. Gradually pour the yeast mixture and milk into the flour, and mix until combined. Increase speed somewhat and knead the dough for about 5 minutes, adding more flour a tablespoon at a time until the ball of dough clears the bottom and sides of the bowl. Remove the dough from the bowl. Clean the bowl and spray with oil, or grease it lightly.

4. Return the dough to the bowl, and turn the dough over a few times to cover it with oil. Cover the bowl with plastic wrap and a clean dish towel, and place the bowl in a draft-free place until the dough has doubled in size, about two hours.

5. Turn the dough out on a lightly floured surface; punch down the dough to flatten it, cover it with a towel, and let it rest for 10 minutes.

6. Grease three 8" x 4" x 2" loaf pans.

7. Divide the dough into three portions. Knead each portion a few times, and then form into loaves. Place each loaf in a greased 8" x 4" x 2" loaf pan. Cover each pan with plastic wrap and towel, and let the dough rise in a draft-free place until almost doubled in size, about one hour.

8. Preheat the oven to 400 degrees F. Bake the bread for 35–40 minutes or until browned and hollow sounding when the bottom of the loaf is tapped. If you have an instant-read thermometer, the interior temperature should be about 190 degrees F.

This versatile dough may be wrapped in plastic wrap after the first rising and refrigerated for a day or two, or frozen for later use.

* If kneading by hand, follow steps 1 and 2, using any large bowl for step 1. After proofing the yeast, gradually add the yeast mixture into the flour and knead the dough, adding more flour a tablespoon at a time until the ball of dough clears the bottom and sides of the bowl. Remove the dough to a lightly floured surface and knead until smooth and elastic, about 5 minutes. Return the dough to the greased bowl, and continue with step 4.

Dried Figs and Stewed Figs

While some figs do grow in Narnia, figs mostly come from Archenland and Calormen. In this world figs are a very popular food and have been for centuries. They are a rich, sweet, and extremely nutritious fruit. It is said, in fact, that with dried figs, bread, wine, olives, and olive oil, you could live a healthy life (though it might be a bit boring). There are two kinds of dried figs: the dessert fig, which is sugary and very sweet, and the ordinary dried fig, which doesn't taste as good but is just as good for you. Stewed figs are also very nice; they are often eaten for breakfast and are said to be good for the digestion. In Narnia both sweet and ordinary dried figs are available.

They investigated the saddle-bags and the results were cheering—a meat pasty, only slightly stale, a lump of dried figs and another lump of green cheese, a little flask of wine, and some money.

—The Horse and His Boy

1 pound dried figs, stems removed

Zest of ½ lemon with no white pith attached

3–4" stick cinnamon

¼ cup granulated sugar or to taste

Pinch of salt

1 cup orange juice

Dried Figs

Dried figs are delicious eaten alone. They are sugary and very sweet and quite a satisfying snack. Stuff a fig with a lump of goat cheese for a special treat.

Stewed Figs

Combine all ingredients in a saucepan, and add enough water to cover the figs by ½". Bring to a boil; then lower heat to a simmer, cover, and cook until the figs are plump and tender. The cooking time will vary depending on the dryness of the fruit. Begin checking after 20 minutes by pricking one with a fork. Cool. These can be served chilled or at room temperature.

ENGLISH OMELETTE

Omelettes can be made with all kinds of things to flavor them. We have suggested several here, but the variety you can make is limited only by your own imagination. Narnian omelettes are made with all kinds of fillings and different kinds of eggs. Wild seagulls' and wild plovers' eggs are two tasty varieties, though, of course, it is always bad manners to serve any egg dish in the presence of Narnian Talking Birds. Omelettes are often regarded as breakfast food but can, in fact, be eaten at any time of the day. Experiment with your omelette recipes by adding spices, such as a touch of curry powder or some ginger, for example.

"So first of all he has porridge and pavenders and kidneys and bacon and omelettes and cold ham and toast and marmalade, and coffee and beer."
—THE SILVER CHAIR

1. Preheat broiler.

2. Stir the water and the egg yolks vigorously until well combined. Stir in a pinch of salt and pepper.

3. Whisk the egg whites until stiff. Gently fold the egg whites into the yolks until just combined.

4. Over medium heat, melt the butter in an oven-proof omelette pan. Tip the pan from side to side to coat well with the butter. Pour in the egg mixture. As the edges set, lift them away from the sides of the pan and let the uncooked egg run under. When the bottom is well set, put the pan under the broiler and cook a minute or so to set the top.

5. Remove the pan from the broiler; spread filling over 1/2 of the omelette. Run a spatula around the edge of the pan, fold the omelette in half, and slide out onto a warm plate. Serve piping hot.

1 SERVING

1 tablespoon water
2 eggs, the yolks separated from the whites
Pinch of salt and white pepper
1 tablespoon butter

ASSORTED FILLINGS:

2 tablespoons grated Cheddar or Cheshire or another flavorful cheese
herbs: 1 tablespoon finely chopped fresh parsley, chives, or dill
onion: 1 tablespoon chopped, sautéed in 1 teaspoon butter until soft and translucent
mushrooms: 2 tablespoons sliced, cooked in 1 teaspoon butter

9

LUNCH

Jack was fascinated by words, and the origin of the word *lunch* is quite interesting. It probably comes from the Middle English word *noneschench* (*none* meaning "noon" plus *schench* meaning "drink"), so originally it seems that lunch would have been a break for a drink in the middle of the day. Nowadays, of course, we make a meal of it. In some parts of the world lunch is the main meal of the day, and many people have a big midday meal on Sundays. At Jack's Oxford home, The Kilns, lunch was served at one o'clock in the afternoon and was a relatively light meal. In Narnia lunch dishes vary according to the season of the year as well as which creatures are eating it. For Naiads and Dryads, the spirits of waters and trees, lunch would be very different from that enjoyed by Dwarfs or eagles, for example. The lunch suggestions we have used here are, naturally enough, those suitable for us.

ROAST LEG OF LAMB

Roast lamb is one of the most delicious of all meats when properly cooked and served. A couple of slices of cold leftover lamb served with mint sauce, hot green peas, and perhaps a few new potatoes is a wonderful lunch. When new potatoes are boiled, a sprig of mint should be added to the water. Lamb and mint traditionally go together, and you'll find they are delicious.

Sheep are very hardy creatures and can live and thrive in country where cattle could not survive. For this reason lamb became popular in mountainous and semidesert areas throughout the world. In Archenland, and throughout the mountains of Scotland, England, Wales, and Ireland, to this day you will see sheep everywhere. Jack got his taste for lamb from his childhood in northern Ireland and England. In Narnia lamb is a favorite dish of the Telmarines.

The Faun trotted in, half dancing, with a tray in its hands which was nearly as large as itself.

—*THE HORSE AND HIS BOY*

6 SERVINGS

1 leg of lamb, 7–9 pounds
2 tablespoons honey
2 cloves garlic (or more to taste), slivered
Leaves of 2 sprigs fresh rosemary, chopped, or 1 teaspoon dried

1. Preheat the oven to 350 degrees F.

2. Place the leg of lamb in a roasting pan. Brush with a thin coating of honey. Cut slits in the lamb, and tuck in slivers of garlic and bits of herbs.

3. Scatter any extra garlic and herbs over the lamb; sprinkle with salt and pepper, and roast uncovered for about 20 minutes per pound.

4. Remove from the oven and allow to sit for 15–20 minutes if serving hot, in order to make carving easier.

5. Slice the lamb and serve with mint sauce on the side. To serve cold, allow the meat to cool completely in the refrigerator.

Lamb can also be roasted in a cooking bag, which you can buy in a grocery store or supermarket. Season as above and place in the bag, following the manufacturer's directions for use.

Leaves of 4 sprigs fresh thyme, chopped, or 1 teaspoon dried
Salt and freshly ground black pepper
Mint sauce (p. 14)

♦

13

COLD LAMB AND GREEN PEAS

"It's lovely," said Lucy, and so it was; an omelette, piping hot, cold lamb and green peas, a strawberry ice, lemon squash to drink with the meal and a cup of chocolate to follow.
—*THE VOYAGE OF THE DAWN TREADER*

6 SERVINGS

12 slices cold roast lamb,
  or more if desired
2 pounds fresh young
  peas, shelled, about 1½
  cups, or one 10-ounce
  package frozen baby
  peas, thawed
1 teaspoon salt
Sprig of mint
1 tablespoon butter
Salt and freshly ground
  black pepper to taste
Mint sauce (see recipe
  below)

1 cup fresh mint leaves
½ cup malt vinegar
¼ cup water
2–3 tablespoons granulated
  sugar (see note)
Pinch of salt

1. Arrange the slices of meat on a serving platter.

2. Bring to a boil enough water to just cover the peas. Add the peas, the salt, and the sprig of mint. Lower heat to a simmer and cook until tender, about 5 minutes for young peas, less for thawed peas.

3. Drain and dress with butter and salt and pepper to taste. Serve hot.

4. Serve the lamb with the mint sauce on the side.

Mint Sauce

1. Wash the mint leaves and chop finely.

2. In a small saucepan, combine the vinegar, water, sugar, and salt and bring to a boil, stirring until the sugar is dissolved. Stir in the mint and simmer for 5 minutes. Taste and adjust seasoning if needed.

3. Serve at room temperature in a small jug with a spoon.

Note: Substitute 3 tablespoons of wildflower honey for the granulated sugar to add a tangy flavor to the mint.

PIGEON PIE

When I was a boy at The Kilns, there were wild wood pigeons that often raided our vegetable garden for anything they could find. It soon became my job to try to keep them under control with a shotgun, and I was a very proud boy when the cook served a pigeon pie for dinner. Cold pigeon pie is delicious for lunches too. In country areas of England and Ireland, you can still get pigeon pie now and then. For America, we have substituted Cornish game hens, which taste very similar. Narnians don't have shotguns, and so Dwarfs and Telmarines hunt with longbows. Shooting a bird on the wing with an arrow takes a great deal of skill, however, so most castles have their own dovecotes, in which pigeons are bred for the table. Pigeon pie is regularly on the menu at Castle Anvard and Cair Paravel.

"Sir, be pleased to take another breast of pigeon, I entreat you."
—THE SILVER CHAIR

1. Remove the meat of Cornish hens from the bones and skin in pieces as large as possible and set aside.

2. In a large saucepan, combine the bones and skin with the water, celery, onion, carrot, thyme, bay leaf, 2 teaspoons salt, and white pepper. Bring to a simmer and cook, covered, for 1 hour. Strain the stock, discarding the solids, and set aside. If time permits, refrigerate the stock and remove the fat. Otherwise skim off as much fat as possible before continuing.

6 SERVINGS

STOCK:

- 2 Cornish game hens, 2½-3 pounds total
- 2 quarts water, or enough to cover bones
- 1 celery rib, cut into large pieces

1 onion, halved
1 carrot, cut into large
  pieces
½ teaspoon dried thyme
1 bay leaf
2 teaspoons salt
½ teaspoon white pepper

PIE:

2 slices bacon, cut in 1"
  pieces
1 tablespoon butter
1 onion, chopped
½ pound lean top-round
  beef, cubed
½ cup burgundy wine
Salt and freshly ground
  black pepper
½ teaspoon dried marjo-
  ram or 1 tablespoon
  minced fresh parsley
2 hard-boiled eggs
1 recipe short pastry (see
  recipe opposite)
2 tablespoons milk

3. Grease a 2-quart casserole and cover the bottom with the bacon.

4. In a nonstick pan, melt the butter and sauté the onion slowly until tender and translucent. Do not brown. Remove the pan from the heat and sprinkle the onion over the bacon in the casserole. Return the pan to the stove, raise the heat, and brown the beef on all sides. Layer the beef over the onion. In the same pan, brown the meat of the Cornish hens, adding more butter if necessary, and add it to the casserole.

5. Add the wine to the pan and deglaze it, loosening all bits of beef and hens. Pour all over the ingredients in the casserole. Add the stock to almost cover the meats. Sprinkle with salt, pepper, and marjoram or parsley. Peel and slice the hard-boiled eggs and arrange on top of all.

6. Preheat the oven to 400 degrees F.

7. Roll out the pastry to about 1/4" thickness and slightly larger than the top of the casserole. Cut out a small circle from the center of the dough. Moisten the rim of the casserole, and fit the pastry over the top, pressing the pastry firmly to the casserole and crimping decoratively. Brush the pastry with milk. Leftover dough can be wrapped well and frozen.

8. Bake the pie for 15 minutes; then lower heat to 275 degrees F and bake for 45 minutes. Remove from the oven and let sit for 10 minutes before serving.

◆

16

Short Pastry

2 SINGLE CRUSTS

1. Combine the flour, sugar, and salt.

2. With a pastry cutter or knife, cut the shortening into the flour mixture until it resembles coarse meal.

3. Using a fork, mix in 5 tablespoons of water. Add more water if necessary to form the dough into a ball. Working the dough as little as possible, form into a disk. Wrap and refrigerate for 1 hour or until ready to roll out. This can be frozen for later use.

2 cups all-purpose flour
1 teaspoon granulated sugar
1 teaspoon salt
3/4 cup lard, or 12 tablespoons vegetable shortening, cold
5 tablespoons water, plus more as needed

MEAT PASTY

If you have to go on a long journey on horseback (suppose you were a messenger for High King Peter or something), there is nothing more delicious to take in your saddlebags than a meat pasty. They are also very nutritious and will keep you in the saddle hour after hour. If you do have to put one in a saddlebag, try wrapping it in fresh grape leaves to keep it moist and good. I like to eat mine with mustard or a touch of hot chili sauce. It will be rare indeed to find a traveling Dwarf, Faun, or Centaur without a few meat pasties to keep him going. Meat pasties are not only good wayfaring provender but are also a delicious meal to enjoy at home.

The next job, clearly, was to get something to eat and drink.
—THE HORSE AND HIS BOY

10 PASTIES

½ pound lean top-round beef
2 small potatoes, peeled and cut into ¼" cubes, about ¾ cup
1 tablespoon butter
1 clove garlic, minced
1 small onion, chopped, about ¼ cup
2 tablespoons chopped parsley
Salt and pepper
1 recipe short pastry (p. 17)
1 large egg, beaten with 1 tablespoon water

1. Mince the beef with a sharp knife, or cut into cubes and process in a food processor until very coarsely chopped.

2. In a medium saucepan, bring to a boil enough salted water to barely cover the potatoes. Add the potatoes, return to the boil, and cook about 10 seconds. Drain and rinse with cold water to stop cooking.

3. In a small frying pan, melt the butter, and add the garlic and onion. Cook over medium heat until translucent and tender. Do not brown.

4. In a medium-size bowl, combine the meat, potatoes, garlic, onion, and parsley. Add salt and pepper.

5. Preheat the oven to 400 degrees F, and grease a baking sheet.

6. On a lightly floured surface, roll out the pastry to ¼" thickness. Cut out rounds of dough about 4½" in diameter. Combine scraps of dough, reroll, and cut. Brush the edges of each round with the

egg wash. Divide the filling among the rounds, making each portion into a well-packed ball. Fold each pasty into a half round, and seal the edges firmly with your fingers, stretching dough slightly if necessary. Place the pasties on the baking sheet, and pierce the top of each pasty with a skewer or fork to let out steam.

7. Bake for 10 minutes. Reduce heat to 325 degrees F, and bake an additional 30 minutes. Serve immediately or remove to rack to cool.

Meat pasties are delicious at room temperature. After they have cooled, they may be wrapped and frozen. To serve, thaw and warm slightly in a microwave or conventional oven.

◆

COLD HAM

A properly cured, well-smoked ham, roasted and glazed, is a delight to the taste and the eye. People started to eat ham and bacon when they discovered, way back in the Dark Ages, that if you salted pork and hung it in the smoke from your cottage fire, it would keep through the winter and you would have bacon for breakfast and ham for dinner through the long, cold, dark months. Dwarfs are the best ham curers in Narnia, and because there are no Talking Pigs it is quite safe to eat ham there.

When the meal (which was pigeon pie, cold ham, salad, and cakes) had been brought, and all had drawn their chairs up to the table and begun, the Knight continued.

—THE SILVER CHAIR

PER PERSON:

2 or 3 thick slices leftover boiled ham (p. 56)
1 cup tender lettuce leaves, torn into bite-size pieces
Sprigs of watercress
Mustard or chutney
Vinaigrette (see recipe below)

4 tablespoons salad oil
2 tablespoons tarragon vinegar
1 tablespoon finely chopped fresh parsley
Salt and pepper to taste

1. Trim the excess fat from the ham.

2. Arrange the lettuce on a plate and top with slices of meat.

3. Garnish with watercress.

4. Serve with mustard or chutney, and the vinaigrette on the side.

Vinaigrette
Whisk all ingredients together and serve.

COLD HAM ROLLS

1. Slice open the baguette lengthwise, leaving one long edge attached.

2. Open flat. Spread with butter and arrange ham, cheese, and lettuce, and add condiment(s) of choice.

3. Cut in half crosswise, arrange on a plate, and garnish with watercress or parsley.

PER PERSON:

1 baguette
1 tablespoon butter
2 slices cold cooked ham
  (p. 56)
A generous slice of
  Cheddar cheese
Lettuce leaves
Mayonnaise, mustard, or
  chutney
Sprigs of watercress or
  parsley

EGG AND CHEESE SANDWICHES

Anyone with a large family should get in the habit of keeping fresh hard-boiled eggs in the fridge, or in Narnia in any cool place. When people come into the house, desperate for a snack, you just can't beat a good egg or egg and cheese sandwich. Nowadays we almost always eat chicken eggs, but in the old days many different eggs were eaten; in Narnia they still are. Seagull eggs, plover eggs, duck eggs, goose eggs, and even turkey eggs are all eggs that I have eaten. Goose eggs are so big that you have to boil them for almost fifteen minutes to make them hard-boiled. And if you ever tried to eat a guinea fowl's egg, you would need a hammer to break the shell. For a quick snack at any time, an egg and cheese sandwich is great.

> There were two hard-boiled egg sandwiches, and two cheese sandwiches, and two with some kind of paste in them.
> —*THE LAST BATTLE*

FOR EACH EGG
SANDWICH:

1 large egg
1 tablespoon butter
2 slices bread
1 tablespoon mayonnaise
Salt and freshly ground
  black pepper
1 raw onion, thinly sliced
1 or 2 leaves fresh lettuce

1. Place the egg in a small saucepan and cover with cold water. Bring to a boil, lower heat to simmer, and cook 7 minutes. Remove the egg from the hot water, and cool under cold running water. Crack the shell of the egg all over and peel.

2. Butter 1 slice of bread; spread mayonnaise on the other. Slice the egg and arrange it on the buttered bread. Sprinkle with salt and pepper and onion. Top with lettuce, and cover with the second slice of bread. Cut into halves or quarters.

◆

1. Butter one slice of bread. Spread the second with condiment(s) of choice.

2. Arrange the cheese on the buttered bread, and top with the remaining slice of bread. Cut into halves or quarters.

FOR EACH CHEESE SANDWICH:

1 tablespoon butter
2 slices bread
Mayonnaise, mustard, or
  chutney
2–3 ounces Cheddar,
  Cheshire, or other
  favorite cheese, thinly
  sliced or grated

OTHER SAVORY FILLINGS FOR SANDWICHES:

Canned tuna fish, mixed
  with chopped capers
  and mayonnaise
Minced or ground boiled
  ham, mixed with a little
  chopped sweet pickle
  and mayonnaise
Minced or ground cooked
  chicken, mixed with
  chopped walnuts and
  mayonnaise
Softened cream cheese and
  minced smoked salmon,
  with a little ground
  horseradish or some
  chopped capers
Chopped cooked chicken
  liver mixed with mashed
  hard-boiled egg and
  softened butter, salt,
  and pepper

Assorted Luncheon Salads

The word *salad* comes from Old Provençal French *salada*, a form of the word *salar*, meaning "to season with salt," and indeed a salad without salt is pretty boring. Today, most salads are lettuce based, with perhaps a few other green leaf vegetables suitable to be eaten raw. You can make salads out of all sorts of interesting things: dandelion leaves, tomatoes, and raw onions, for example. In Narnia very often you will find wild wood sorrel, fresh young dandelion leaves, and other woodland and meadow herbs in the salads. There is also a wide variety of salad dressings. Our favorite is an old family recipe called "Gresham Dressing," which is a mixture of equal parts extra virgin olive oil, vinegar, and tomato ketchup. Add salt, pepper, crushed garlic, a touch of sugar to taste, and, if you like, a little chili, and mix thoroughly. It's great!

Before they got into it Shasta dismounted and entered it on foot to buy a loaf and some onions and radishes.

—The Horse and His Boy

6 SERVINGS EACH

6 cups mixed greens, washed, dried, and torn into bite-size pieces: Boston lettuce, red leaf lettuce, romaine, young spinach leaves, arugula, watercress, endive, or other seasonal greens such as dandelion

SALAD CREAM:

4 tablespoons heavy cream or evaporated skim milk
1 tablespoon white wine vinegar
½ teaspoon Dijon mustard
1 teaspoon granulated sugar
Pinch of salt

Green Salad with Salad Cream

1. Place the greens in a salad bowl.

2. Whisk together the cream or milk, vinegar, mustard, sugar, and salt.

3. Right before serving, spoon 2 or 3 tablespoons of the salad cream over the greens; toss lightly. Repeat with additional dressing until leaves are well coated.

24

Tomato Salad with Vinaigrette

1. Slice the tomatoes and arrange them on a serving platter.

2. Scatter the herbs over the tomatoes.

3. Whisk together the olive oil, vinegar, salt, and pepper, and spoon over all.

5 large ripe tomatoes
4 tablespoons finely minced fresh herbs, such as parsley, basil, and mint

VINAIGRETTE:

4 tablespoons extra virgin olive oil
1 tablespoon tarragon vinegar
Salt and freshly ground black pepper to taste

Potato Salad

1. Peel the potatoes and cut into ¼" slices. Put them into a saucepan, cover with water, and add the salt. Bring to a boil and cook until barely tender. Drain and place in a bowl with the red onion.

2. Pour the broth over the potatoes, and let stand a few minutes to begin to absorb broth.

3. Combine the egg yolk*, vinegar, and oil, and pour over the potatoes. Season with salt and pepper, and mix gently to coat potatoes. Serve warm or chilled.

2 pounds potatoes, (about 6 medium potatoes)
1 teaspoon salt
½ cup minced red onion
½ cup chicken broth, warmed
1 egg yolk
6 tablespoons red wine vinegar
6 tablespoons extra virgin olive oil
1 teaspoon salt
A few grinds of black pepper

Quick Potato Salad

Pour all ingredients over the potato cubes and stir gently. Refrigerate and serve chilled.

*If you are concerned about salmonella contamination in raw eggs, leave out the egg yolk and proceed as directed.

6 medium-size potatoes, cooked, peeled, and cut into 3/4" cubes
½ cup finely chopped onion
1 cup mayonnaise
Salt and pepper
3 tablespoons minced fresh parsley or chives

♦

Apples, Herbs, and Cheese

For many years through the ages, men (and Dwarfs and others) working in the fields have needed good nutritious snack foods to keep up their energy during the long, hard days spent farming the land. The snack needs to be something you can carry easily in your pocket or lunch bag, and even today a meal of apples, herbs, and cheese is known in England as a ploughman's lunch. I myself have sat down beside the furrows, eaten my ploughman's lunch, and given my apple core to the horse. Apples and cheese go very well together, and a selection of wild herbs adds just an extra tang of flavor. On a hot summer's day, outside with the breeze in your hair, there is nothing better than a ploughman's lunch washed down with a flask of good cider.

> After lunch, which they had on the terrace (it was cold
> birds and cold game pie and wine and bread and cheese) . . .
> —THE HORSE AND HIS BOY

Apples, quartered and dipped into a quart of water containing 1½ tablespoons of lemon juice

Cheeses, including Cheddar, Cheshire, Gloucester, Stilton, or other favorites

Green and black olives

Herbs, including salad burnet, caraway leaves, fronds of dill and fennel, young spring dandelion leaves, purslane, sorrel, parsley, and watercress

Edible flowers, such as borage, chive, calendula, sage, thyme, and sweet violets

Water biscuits, or any selection of your favorite crackers

Arrange bite-size fingers or wedges of cheese on a platter with the olives. Garnish with herbs and flowers, and serve with apples and water biscuits.

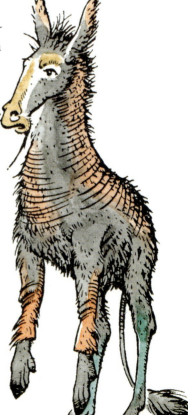

AFTERNOON TEA

In England, as in many other parts of the world, the consumption of food often has traditions attached to it. When I was a child at The Kilns, we had breakfast around eight A.M., "elevenses" at eleven, lunch at one P.M., afternoon tea at four, dinner at seven, and finally, if we were still hungry, supper at around ten thirty. Elevenses consisted of a cup of tea and a couple of cookies, or biscuits as we called them. Afternoon tea was a much more serious affair and was traditionally divided into two types: tea and high tea. Tea could be anything from a simple cup of tea and a biscuit to tea, biscuits, cakes, and maybe even little meat sandwiches. High tea, on the other hand, would be much more elaborate, consisting of a light meal served with a cup of tea, and would often be eaten if for some reason one had to miss out on dinner. The high tea would keep you going until you had the opportunity to have a rather larger than usual late supper. Narnian high teas are a delicious mixture of foods. The tea that Mr. Tumnus served to Lucy is a pretty good example. If you come to England, or to Narnia, it is very likely that someone will invite you to tea. If they do, you will probably enjoy yourself very much.

Boiled Eggs and Scotch Eggs

B oiled eggs are eaten all over the world, and in Narnia, too. Many different eggs can be used, but these days we mostly use chicken eggs. Some people like their eggs soft-boiled and some hard-boiled, but the way they are eaten varies from place to place. In America people tend to peel the shell off the whole egg and just eat it. In England and Narnia the egg is usually put into an egg cup, the top chopped off with a knife, and the egg eaten out of its shell with an egg spoon, though nowadays most people just use a teaspoon. Scotch eggs are absolutely delicious and filled with protein and vitamins. Cold Scotch eggs are also used by Dwarfs and others as easily carried traveling food.

There was a nice brown egg, lightly boiled, for each of them.
—The Lion, the Witch and the Wardrobe

PER PERSON:

1 large egg
1 teaspoon butter
Salt and pepper

Boiled Egg

1. Place the egg in a saucepan with water to cover. Bring to a gentle boil, and cook 3 minutes for a soft-boiled egg, 4 minutes to set the white, and 5–6 minutes to set the egg firmly.

2. Lift the egg from the water, and set wide end up in an egg cup. As you crack and peel your egg, you may add butter, salt, and pepper to taste.

6 SERVINGS

6 hard-boiled eggs, peeled
  and chilled
3/4 pounds sausage meat
  (p. 72)
1 uncooked egg
1 cup fresh bread crumbs
Vegetable oil

Scotch Eggs

1. Divide the sausage meat into 6 portions, and press 1 portion around each cooked egg to cover completely.

2. Beat the uncooked egg; then roll each sausage-covered egg first in the beaten egg, and then in the bread crumbs.

3. Heat a 1/2" of oil in a sauté pan. The oil should be hot enough to brown a 1-inch cube of bread in 40–50 seconds. It should not be smoking hot. Add the eggs, turning them often to brown the meat and cook it thoroughly. If the oil begins to smoke, reduce heat slightly so the meat cooks completely while browning on the outside.

4. Drain on paper towels and serve hot.

◆

A Lovely Cup of Hot Tea

The traditions of tea drinking go back thousands of years and started in ancient China. Water had to be boiled to make it healthy, but it didn't really taste very good, so they began to put herbs in it, and soon tea leaves were found to impart a beautiful fragrance and flavor to the hot water. When the English discovered China, they also discovered tea and took it home with them. There are many different kinds of tea today, and most are grown in India, Sri Lanka (Ceylon), and China. The flavor of each tea varies enormously depending on what variety it is and where it is from. People take their tea in a number of different ways: Some take it with milk and some take it with milk and sugar, while others prefer theirs black with lemon. Tea is very refreshing and satisfying. Jack was a great tea drinker, preferring good Ceylon teas.

> *How Aslan provided food for them all I don't know;*
> *but somehow or other they found themselves all sitting down*
> *on the grass to a fine high tea at about eight o'clock.*
> —THE LION, THE WITCH AND THE WARDROBE

Cold water
1 teaspoon tea leaves per cup of tea, plus a teaspoonful for the pot
A teapot of suitable size
Granulated sugar
Lemon slices
Cream or milk

1. Fill an empty tea kettle with cold water and bring to a boil.

2. Pour about a cup of boiling water into the teapot; let it heat the pot for a minute or two, and then discard it.

3. Add the tea leaves to the pot, and pour in a cup of boiling water for each cup of tea. Place the cover on the teapot, and allow to steep 3–4 minutes, or until the tea reaches the desired strength.

4. Pour the tea through a tea strainer into a teacup, and serve with sugar, lemon, cream, or milk.*

*Don't try to mix milk or cream with lemon in the tea, or it will curdle and it will be disgusting.

HOT SARDINES ON TOAST

Sardines are little tiny fish very popular in England. They are very tasty and can be eaten hot or cold. I like them with a dash of hot chili sauce. Sardines used to be caught in huge numbers off the coast of California. In Narnia they are commonly caught off the Calormene coast by both the Calormen and Lone Islands fishing fleets.

That evening after tea the four children all managed
to get down to the beach again and get their shoes and
stockings off and feel the sand between their toes.
—THE LION, THE WITCH AND THE WARDROBE

1. Toast the bread, and butter lightly.

2. In a small sauté pan, heat the sardines in a little of their own oil.

3. Top the toast with sardines, and sprinkle with a few drops of lemon juice and a little pepper.

2 SERVINGS

4 slices bread
Butter
1 tin sardines
Fresh lemon juice
Freshly ground black
  pepper

31

SUGAR-TOPPED CAKE

As you know, there are lots of different cakes that can be sugar frosted. Mr. Tumnus served the kind that we have included here, though I'm sure he could make other cakes as well (Fauns are good cooks). I like this cake not only because it tastes so good, but also because it is very nutritious. One of the lesser-known uses for a piece of nice cake like this is to fry a slice (about half an inch thick) in a little butter and have it for breakfast on a cold winter's morning. It is a Dwarf's delight.

And when Lucy was tired of eating, the Faun began to talk. He had wonderful tales to tell of life in the forest.
—*The Lion, the Witch and the Wardrobe*

ONE 8" ROUND CAKE

2¼ cups all-purpose flour
1 teaspoon baking powder
½ teaspoon salt
12 tablespoons (1½ sticks) butter
¾ cup granulated sugar
3 large eggs
½ cup milk
1 cup raisins, chopped
½ cup currants
¼ cup candied orange peel, chopped fine
¼ cup blanched almonds, chopped
Sugar Cake Frosting (see recipe opposite)
Candied cherries (optional)

1. Preheat the oven to 325 degrees F. Grease an 8" x 2" round pan, and line the bottom with a circle of parchment paper or waxed paper.

2. Sift together the flour, baking powder, and salt.

3. With an electric mixer or by hand, cream the butter and sugar together until fluffy. Add the eggs one at a time, beating well after each addition.

4. Add the flour mixture to the butter and sugar alternately with the milk, beating just until mixed.

5. Fold in the fruit and nuts.

6. Pour the batter into the greased pan.

7. Bake for 1 hour 15 minutes, until nicely browned and quite firm to the touch.

8. Cool in the pan for 10 minutes. Remove to a rack and cool completely. Remove the cake from the pan, and frost with sugar cake frosting. Decorate with candied cherries if desired.

◆

Sugar Cake Frosting

1. Beat the egg whites until they form stiff, shiny peaks. Continue to beat while adding the vinegar, lemon juice, and salt.

2. Sift the cornstarch and sugar together, and beat in gradually until frosting is of spreading consistency.

ABOUT 2 CUPS

2 large egg whites*
2 teaspoons white wine
    vinegar
1 teaspoon lemon juice
Dash salt
2 teaspoons cornstarch
1½ cups confectioners'
    sugar, sifted, plus more
    if needed

*If salmonella is a
    concern, you may use
    powdered egg whites,
    reconstituted according to
    package directions.

OATCAKES

Oatcakes go back to the dim Dark Ages in Scotland, where the weather in many places makes it almost impossible to grow anything but oats. In cold, damp, misty Scotland, you need good high-energy food, and oatcakes are perfect. While they are delicious for afternoon tea, they are also good saddlebag supplies, giving you energy and strength to ride on when you are sent out on the High King's business.

As it was now past the middle of the day, they rested with the centaurs and ate such foods as the centaurs provided—cakes of oaten meal, and apples, and herbs, and wine, and cheese.

—PRINCE CASPIAN

36 OATCAKES

2 cups all-purpose flour
½ teaspoon salt
½ teaspoon baking soda
6 tablespoons butter (¾ stick), room temperature
6 tablespoons lard, room temperature
2 cups rolled oats, not instant
½ cup granulated sugar, plus more if needed
4 tablespoons milk

1. Preheat the oven to 400 degrees F. Grease a baking sheet.

2. Sift together the flour, salt, and baking soda.

3. Rub in the butter and lard with your fingers until well combined. The butter and lard will almost disappear into the flour. Mix in the oats and the sugar, adding more sugar if desired.

4. Mix in the milk and knead dough until it holds together. Roll out ¼" thick and cut out small rounds. Place on the greased baking sheet.

5. Bake for 10 minutes until the oatcakes just begin to color. Cool on a rack.

♦

Risen Oatcakes

1. Oil a large bowl, and grease a baking sheet.

2. Mix the rolled oats, lard, and sugar. Knead the mixture into the bread dough. Form into a ball, place in the oiled bowl, cover with plastic wrap, and allow to sit for 30 minutes.

3. Preheat the oven to 400 degrees F. Roll out the dough between sheets of parchment paper to ¼" thickness or as thin as possible. Cut into 36 squares and place on the prepared baking sheet. Sprinkle with salt.

4. Bake immediately for 10–12 minutes, until light brown. Remove to rack to cool.

Serve plain or with cheese or butter. Oatcakes are also delicious served with honey or strawberry jam topped with a dollop of heavy cream that has been sweetened with confectioners' sugar or honey.

ABOUT 36 OATCAKES

2 cups rolled oats, not instant
¼ cup lard, melted
⅓ cup granulated sugar
8 ounces risen white bread dough, about ⅓ of the recipe (p. 6), at room temperature
1 teaspoon salt

♦

DINNER

Dinner is the main meal of the day. At The Kilns it would be served at seven in the evening and could be either a very simple meal or an elaborate feast, depending on the occasion. At Cair Paravel things are much the same. Some dinners are merely family meals with the kings and queens, while others are full state banquets. The recipes we have selected would be suitable for either of these kinds of occasions, though turkey, venison, and pheasant might be for a more formal occasion. In medieval times, as in Narnia, dinners were often great complicated affairs, lasting for many hours. A king would want to show off his wealth by providing many courses of exquisitely prepared food. In Narnia state banquets are a bit more restrained. Delicious foods are served but not to the extent of ostentation. Traditionally, throughout the history of the world, wine has been served with fine food. Narnia is known for its wonderful wines, because Bacchus, the ancient Greek god of wine, spends quite a lot of his time there and ensures that all Narnian wines are good wines.

Good Narnian dinners usually consist of three or four courses. Most begin with soup, followed by the main course (either meat or fish with vegetables and/or salad), then a dessert, and perhaps finishing off with a cup of coffee. Some people like to have chocolate or mints at the end of a meal. I prefer to serve something sharp in flavor, like a sorbet or a small, natural citrus fruit salad with pieces of orange, lemon, and grapefruit softened by a sweet, clear Grand Marnier sauce, for example.

I think it would be great fun to have a Narnian dinner party. You could invite a few friends, tell them to dress up as their favorite Narnian character, and then serve a Cair Paravel banquet. This next section will give you some recipe ideas for your party.

COCK-A-LEEKIE SOUP

L eek soup is a traditional dish in Scotland and Wales. Around the beginning of the nineteenth century, the Scots started to add a chicken to the pot for flavor, and that is the way the Narnians like it. The leek is the badge of Wales, said to have been introduced to that part of Britain by St. David. For some reason I don't understand, Narnian, Welsh, and Scottish leeks seem to have a sharper flavor than those grown in England. Keen gardeners in England, and perhaps Archenland, have been able to produce gigantic specimens, up to three feet long and three inches thick. Cock-a-leekie soup is delicious and contains almost all the nutritional substances you need to live on. It can be a meal in itself.

The meal—which I suppose we must call dinner, though it was nearer tea time—was cock-a-leekie soup, and hot roast turkey, and a steamed pudding, and roast chestnuts, and as much fruit as you could eat.

—THE SILVER CHAIR

8-10 SERVINGS

1 large carrot, about ½ pound
1 white turnip, about ½ pound
1 large onion
6–8 whole cloves
1 bunch leeks, about 2 pounds
1 chicken, 4½–5 pounds
½ cup rice
1 tablespoon salt
1 teaspoon white pepper
12 pitted prunes
Finely chopped fresh parsley for garnish

1. Wash and trim the carrot and turnip; halve and place in a large stock pot. Peel the loose skin off the onion, wash, halve, and stud each half with cloves. Add to the pot. Cut the tough green tops off the leeks, and wash each leaf carefully to remove sand. Add to the pot. Set aside the tender white bases until step 3.

2. Wash the chicken thoroughly inside and out, and place on top of the vegetables. Add water to just cover the chicken, 4–5 quarts depending on the size of the pot. Bring to a boil; then reduce heat, cover, and simmer until chicken is very tender, about 2 hours. Remove the chicken from the pot. Strain the broth, discarding solids. If time permits, refrigerate the broth and chicken overnight or until the fat congeals, and you can remove the solid fat the next day. Otherwise skim off as much fat as possible, and proceed with the recipe.

3. Halve the whites of the leeks lengthwise, separate into leaves, and wash carefully to remove all sand. Slice into ¼" pieces.

4. Return 8 cups of defatted chicken broth to the stockpot, reserving any extra broth for another use. Bring to a simmer and add the leeks, rice, seasonings, and prunes. Cook about 20 minutes or until the rice is tender.

5. While the leeks and rice are cooking, remove half of the meat from the chicken, discarding the fat, bones, and skin. Cut the meat into bite-size pieces, and add to the soup to reheat. Reserve the remaining chicken for another use.

6. Taste the soup for seasoning, adding salt and pepper if necessary. Ladle into individual plates or a tureen and garnish with parsley.

MUSHROOM SOUP

Mushroom soup is another good, rich soup that serves as an excellent first course for a dinner. Mushrooms have been eaten for thousands of years, but before you go out and pick any, make sure you know exactly what to pick and what to avoid, as some mushrooms are deadly poisonous. Narnia has many species of edible mushrooms, but also quite a few poisonous ones. The people of the Toadstools, called by the White Witch when summoning her army, are the evil spirits of poisonous mushrooms, just as Dryads are the spirits of good trees. Jack loved mushrooms, and this is an excellent recipe for a delicious mushroom soup.

They progressed up the long dining-hall in a series of bounds or jumps. . . . When the dish contained anything like soup or stew the result was rather disastrous.
—*THE VOYAGE OF THE DAWN TREADER*

6 SERVINGS

1½ pounds fresh mush-
  rooms—field mushrooms
  or portobello if possible
  (see note)
1 tablespoon butter or
  olive oil
¼ cup chopped shallots
1 teaspoon finely chopped
  garlic
½ cup dry white wine
8 cups chicken broth
1 cup heavy cream
Salt and white pepper
Pinch of nutmeg
¼ cup finely chopped
  fresh parsley
2 tablespoons butter (¼
  stick), optional
¼ cup dry sherry, optional

1. Clean and slice the mushrooms.

2. In a large pot, heat the butter or oil and sauté the shallots and garlic until translucent. Do not brown. Add the mushrooms and cook, stirring now and then, for about 10 minutes.

3. Stir in the wine and chicken broth and bring to a boil. Reduce heat and simmer for 30 minutes. Remove from heat and allow to cool slightly.

4. In a blender, puree the soup in small batches. Return the soup to the pot. Stir in the heavy cream.

5. Just before serving, reheat the soup until very hot but not boiling. Season to taste with salt, pepper, and nutmeg. Swirl in butter, if desired, and ladle into individual soup plates or a tureen.

6. Sprinkle with parsley and add sherry, if desired.

Cure for warts: wash in a silver basin by moonlight.

Note: Be sure you know which varieties of field mushrooms are nonpoisonous, if you plan to pick them. Otherwise, many supermarkets package edible field mushrooms.

TRADITIONAL ROAST TURKEY

The turkey, an American bird, was introduced to England during the reign of Henry VIII. Wild turkeys used to be plentiful in North America. Turkey has become traditional for Thanksgiving in America and Christmas in England and America. Today turkeys are raised almost entirely indoors, but they actually taste much better if they can run free in the woods and fields. There are two recipes for stuffing here. Both are tasty, but the chestnut stuffing is much preferred by Narnian folk, particularly the Giants of Harfang, who have some strange tastes but know how to cook.

> "Lie there, your Highness, and I will bring you up a
> little feast to yourself in a few moments."
> —THE HORSE AND HIS BOY

8–10 SERVINGS

1 oven-ready turkey, about
   12 pounds
Salt and freshly ground
   pepper
1 lemon
Stuffing (pp. 44–45); it is
   common to use two
   kinds, putting the richer
   one in the smaller neck
   cavity
4 tablespoons (½ stick)
   butter, softened
1 cup water
Gravy (p. 45)

1. Preheat the oven to 350 degrees F. Oil a roasting pan.

2. Remove the package of giblets from the turkey and set aside. Wash the turkey thoroughly inside and out with cold water, and pat dry with paper towels. Season the cavities with salt and pepper. Cut the lemon in half and rub the cavities with the cut side of one half.

3. Spoon the stuffing into the body of the turkey, filling the cavity but not packing it too tightly, as stuffing will expand as it cooks. Tuck the legs back under the flap of skin to close the opening, or secure with skewers and string. Stuff the neck cavity, and bend the wings back under the turkey to hold the neck skin closed or skewer and tie. If using two kinds of stuffing, put the bread stuffing in the large cavity and the chestnut stuffing in the neck. The remaining bread stuffing can be baked in a buttered casserole dish during the last 45 minutes or so as the turkey roasts.

4. Place the turkey in the oiled roasting pan. Rub the butter over the skin, making sure to coat the breastbone, wings, and legs. Squeeze juice from remaining lemon half over all, and season with salt and pepper.

5. Pour the water into bottom of the pan. Cover the pan with its own lid or a tent of heavy-duty foil.

6. Roast for 4 hours, or 20 minutes per pound. Remove the lid; baste with pan juices. Raise the oven temperature to 425 degrees F, and roast until nicely browned, about 20 minutes more. When the turkey is fully cooked, an instant-read thermometer inserted into the thickest part of the thigh meat will read 190 degrees F.

7. Remove the turkey to a warmed platter; tent it with foil and allow it to sit while you finish the gravy.

The turkey may also be roasted in an oven bag, following the instructions included with the bag. This shortens the cooking time somewhat.

2 pounds chestnuts
Chicken broth to cover
4 tablespoons (½ stick)
   butter
¼ teaspoon salt
4 or 5 grindings of pepper
Pinch of ground cinnamon
½ teaspoon granulated
   sugar

Chestnut Stuffing

1. With a sharp knife, cut a cross on the flat side of each chestnut, trying not to cut into the flesh of the nut.

2. Place the nuts in a pot with the broth and simmer for about 20 minutes. Lift the nuts from the broth with a slotted spoon and cool slightly.

3. When the chestnuts are cool enough to handle, remove the shell and peel off the inner skin. Return them to the broth, and simmer 15 to 20 minutes or until they are tender enough to mash easily.

4. Drain the nuts, reserving the broth, and mash or rice them.

5. Mix in the butter, salt, pepper, cinnamon, and sugar and enough reserved broth to make a stuffing the consistency of mashed potatoes. Leftover broth can be used in the gravy.

6. Stuff the turkey just before roasting.

Since chestnuts are seasonal, canned whole unsweetened chestnuts may be substituted. A 10-ounce can contains about 40 chestnuts, equal to about 1 pound fresh. They have already been peeled and cooked. Drain them, simmer in chicken broth about 10 minutes, and proceed with step 4.

◆

Bread and Herb Stuffing

1. Melt the butter in a sauté pan over medium-low heat. Stir in the onions and celery and cook until translucent. Do not brown. Transfer to a large bowl.

2. Add the bread cubes to the bowl, and toss to coat with the butter mixture.

3. Combine the milk and egg and stir into the bread mixture. Mix in the parsley, sage, and thyme, or poultry seasoning, and add salt and pepper. The stuffing should be moist but not soggy. Add more milk if necessary.

4. Stuff the turkey just before roasting.

Giblets

1. While the turkey is roasting, rinse the giblets carefully. Place all the ingredients in a saucepan with broth or water to cover.

2. Bring the broth to a boil. Reduce to a simmer, cover pan, and cook for 1 hour. Strain, discarding the vegetables. The meat of the giblets may be diced finely and added to the stuffing or the gravy (see next page) if desired.

4 tablespoons (½ stick) butter
1 onion chopped, about 1½ cups
3 ribs celery, sliced
6 cups stale bread cubes or purchased stuffing mix
½ cup milk
1 egg, beaten
½ cup finely chopped fresh parsley
1 tablespoon each chopped fresh sage and thyme leaves, or 1 tablespoon dried poultry seasoning
Salt and pepper

1 package of giblets from turkey
2 ribs celery, cut in large pieces
1 large onion, chopped, about 1½ cups
1 carrot, washed, cut in large pieces
1 teaspoon salt
Chicken broth or water

GRAVY:

4 tablespoons fat from
  roasting pan drippings
4 tablespoons all-purpose
  or instant flour
3 cups hot giblet broth, or
  giblet broth plus chicken
  broth or liquid from
  cooking vegetables
Salt and white pepper

1. Remove 4 tablespoons of fat from the roasting pan and reserve. Drain off the remaining fat from the roasting pan, leaving the juices and solids in the pan. Return the fat to the pan. With a wooden spoon, scrape the pan to loosen bits of meat. Gradually work the flour into the fat in the pan, and mix until it is a smooth paste.

2. Cook over low heat for 3 or 4 minutes, stirring constantly. Slowly whisk in hot liquid. Simmer 5 minutes. If gravy becomes too thick, add more broth or water to thin.

3. Taste for seasoning, and add salt and pepper if necessary. Serve hot with the roast turkey.

◆

GRILLED LOIN OF VENISON

Venison is a rich, strong meat that hunters often grilled over an open campfire. One man would see to cooking and tending the fire, while the others would sharpen their arrowheads and check their bowstrings for the next day's hunting. In the Middle Ages in England, the deer that ran free in the forests were the property of the king, and Robin Hood and his Merrie Men would get in trouble for taking a deer when they needed one. It is very important to remember that in Narnia one should never shoot an arrow at a Talking Deer. There is no excuse for doing so, because the Talking Deer are bigger than ordinary deer and will soon tell you to leave them alone. Venison is also delicious when stewed with wine and a couple of plums.

Doctor Cornelius quickly cut up the remains of a cold chicken and some slices of venison and put them, with bread and an apple or so and a little flask of good wine, into the wallet which he then gave to Caspian.
—PRINCE CASPIAN

1. Season the steaks with the pepper and the juniper berries.

2. Combine the parsley, chives, and chervil with the butter. Set aside.

3. In a small saucepan over low heat, melt the jelly with the port and keep warm.

6 SERVINGS

6 strip loin steaks of venison, about 5 ounces each
A few grinds of black pepper

47

1 tablespoon crushed
   juniper berries (see note)
1 tablespoon finely
   chopped fresh parsley
1 tablespoon finely
   chopped fresh chives
1 tablespoon finely
   chopped fresh chervil
4 tablespoons (½ stick)
   butter, room temperature
½ cup red currant jelly
2 tablespoons port wine
Sprigs of watercress

4. Grill or broil the steaks until rare or medium rare, 3–4 minutes on each side. Do not overcook.

5. Put the steaks on a warm platter; spread with the herb butter and spoon the red currant–port sauce over them. Garnish with watercress.

Beef or lamb may be substituted if venison is not available.

Note: Juniper berries can be crushed in a mortar with pestle or can be placed in a small plastic bag and crushed with a heavy pan.

ROAST PHEASANT

Pheasants are interesting birds. According to Greek myth, they are said to have been discovered by Jason and the Argonauts on the banks of the river Phasis near Mount Ararat. Nowadays they are common in almost all the southern parts of Narnia, and in Europe. While most of you will not be hunting for your pheasant, you should know that there is some skill in selecting and preparing a pheasant for the table. First of all, the cock (male) bird is thought to be superior in flavor to the hen, but if it has long, sharp spurs on its legs, it is probably too old to eat. Second, for the best flavor the bird should hang in a cool hunter's larder for some time before being dressed. If it is cooked fresh, it will be dry and taste no better than a chicken.

To sleep under the stars, to drink nothing but well water and to live chiefly on nuts and wild fruit was a strange experience for Caspian after his bed with silken sheets in a tapestried chamber at the castle, with meals laid out on gold and silver dishes.

—PRINCE CASPIAN

1. If not acquired oven ready, clean, pluck, and singe pheasants that have hung for 4–5 days.

2. Preheat the oven to 425 degrees F.

3. Wash the pheasants thoroughly inside and out with cold water and pat dry with paper towels. Season with salt and pepper inside and out.

4. Mince the beef and place a portion inside each bird. This prevents the bird from drying out. Wrap each bird with 3 strips of bacon, securing each slice with toothpicks.

5. Roast for 45 minutes. Remove to a heated platter while making the gravy.

6. To serve, cut each bird in half through the breast and backbones with a sharp knife or poultry shears. Arrange on a serving plate with a portion of bread sauce, and drizzle with gravy. Garnish with watercress.

6 SERVINGS

3 young pheasants, about 1⅓ pounds each
Salt and freshly ground pepper
6 ounces stewing beef
9 slices bacon
Gravy (p. 50)
Bread sauce (p. 50)
Sprigs of watercress

49

Butter if necessary
3 tablespoons flour
2 cups chicken broth (or use water in which vegetables have been cooked or plain water if necessary)
Salt and pepper

Gravy

1. Measure the fat and pan drippings. Add butter if necessary to total 4 tablespoons.

2. Work the flour into the roasting pan drippings. Cook for 2 or 3 minutes over low heat.

3. Add the liquid gradually, whisking until the gravy thickens slightly, to make a fairly thin sauce. Add more liquid if needed. Add salt and pepper to taste.

1 onion, washed
6 whole cloves
2 cups milk
1 teaspoon salt
Pinch of cayenne
3/4 cup fine fresh bread crumbs
Pinch of mace
2 tablespoons (1/4 stick) butter
1 tablespoon heavy cream

Bread Sauce

1. Halve the onion and stud each piece with three cloves.

2. In a medium saucepan, bring the milk and salt to a simmer. Add the onion and pepper, and cook for 5 minutes.

3. Stir in the bread crumbs, cover, and simmer 10 minutes. Remove from heat until ready to finish.

4. Just before serving, remove the onion. Stir in the mace, butter, and cream. Taste for seasoning and add salt if desired. Reheat and serve hot.

LOBSTERS AND SALAD

When I was a boy, I used to go out in lobster-fishing boats off Pembrokeshire in South Wales, and there I developed a love for boats and the sea. I still like lobster, too. The lobster is probably the most delicious of all shellfish, and there are many different kinds. The rock lobster (also known as the langouste), which is a kind of brownish-yellow color, is one popular variety, but in my opinion nowhere near as good as the beautiful dark-blue Atlantic clawed lobster. However, neither of these is anywhere near as good as the black Tasmanian freshwater lobster, now fairly rare but once found in any river or stream with a muddy bottom throughout Tasmania. The lobsters of Narnia are most like those found in the Irish Sea: deep blue in color until cooked, when, like all lobsters, they turn bright red.

There were lobsters and salad and snipe stuffed with almonds and truffles, and a complicated dish made of chicken livers and rice and raisins and nuts, and there were cool melons and gooseberry fools and mulberry fools, and every kind of nice thing that can be made with ice.
—THE HORSE AND HIS BOY

1. Bring a very large pot of salted water to a boil, about 1 tablespoon salt per gallon of water. When the water is at a full rolling boil, plunge the lobster in headfirst. Return to the boil, lower heat to medium, and cook uncovered for 7–9 minutes.

2. With long-handled tongs, remove the lobster from the pot to drain. With kitchen shears, cut the shell open from head to tail on the middle of the underside. Pry the shell open and remove the stomach sac near the head and the spongy material along the sides of the body. Remove the dark vein in the tail, if there is one. Leave in the red lobster coral (the roe) and the green tomalley (the liver). Crack the claws with a mallet, and serve immediately with lemon butter,

PER PERSON:

1¼–1½ pounds live lobster
2 tablespoons (¼ stick) butter, melted with 1 teaspoon lemon juice (optional)
Salad and dressing (p. 52)

51

providing a nutcracker and seafood fork or pick to aid in extracting the meat.

3. To serve chilled, cool and refrigerate the lobster. When ready to serve, split it from end to end and remove the stomach and intestinal vein but leave the green tomalley. Crack the claws. Serve as is in the shell, providing a cracker and pick to aid in extracting the meat. Or pick out the meat, cut it into bite-size pieces, and incorporate it into the salad.

If serving lobster whole, make a side plate of salad greens, beets, egg, and tomato. If the lobster meat is removed from the shell, arrange the salad on a larger plate, including the lobster meat. In either case, whisk together the oil, vinegar, mustard, and honey, and stir in the salt and capers. Serve in a small jug with a spoon.

SALAD:

1 cup mixed salad greens
1/4 cup cubed pickled beets
1 hard-boiled egg, chopped
1/2 tomato, chopped

DRESSING:

2 tablespoons salad oil
1 teaspoon vinegar
1 teaspoon Dijon mustard
1/2 teaspoon honey
Pinch of salt
1 tablespoon chopped capers

◆

BOILED CHICKEN

Chickens are often regarded as the most delicate and easy to digest of all animal foods. Certainly it is good food for all of us and especially for anybody who is sick. Narnian Dwarfs would always prepare a chicken to be absolutely delicious.

But it was a good meal otherwise, with mushroom soup and boiled chickens and hot boiled ham . . .
—*THE VOYAGE OF THE DAWN TREADER*

1. Wash the chicken thoroughly inside and out. Cut the lemon in half, and rub the chicken inside and out with the cut sides of the lemon, squeezing juice as you rub. Put the lemon halves into the cavity of the bird, or add them to the pot if the chicken is in pieces. Place the chicken in a pot just large enough to hold all the ingredients. Add the vegetables and seasonings and water or broth to cover.

2. Bring to a boil; then lower to a simmer. Cover the pot and cook for 1 hour or until juices run clear when the fleshy part of the thigh is pierced with a skewer.

6 SERVINGS

1 chicken, whole or jointed, about 4 pounds
1 lemon
1 onion, quartered
1 carrot, scrubbed and cut into large pieces
1 tablespoon chopped fresh thyme, or 1 teaspoon dried
1 tablespoon chopped fresh sage or 1 teaspoon dried

1 bay leaf
1 teaspoon salt
8 peppercorns
*Water or, for a richer
  dish, chicken broth*
Gravy (see recipe below)

*2 tablespoons (¼ stick)
  butter*
½ cup all-purpose flour
3 cups defatted broth
Salt and white pepper

3. If serving hot, remove the chicken to a warm platter and keep warm while making the gravy. To serve cold, allow to cool, then wrap and refrigerate. Strain hot broth and use for gravy or reserve for another use.

Gravy

1. In a medium saucepan, melt the butter and stir in the flour until completely combined. Cook, stirring, for 2 minutes. Slowly whisk in the broth and simmer for 5 minutes.

2. Taste for seasoning, and add salt and pepper as needed. Serve hot.

STEWED EEL

Eels have been eaten for thousands of years all over the world. They can be found in almost any river, stream, pond, or lake that you can imagine. They were a favorite food of the Roman emperors and of kings, queens, nobles, and commoners throughout history. In some parts of England fishermen can still be seen catching eels in eel traps or eel bobs, just as they did when the Romans conquered Britain. To this day eels are considered a great delicacy in many parts of the world. The Marsh-wiggles of Narnia regard them as the very finest food possible. This is one of their recipes.

"You've got to learn that life isn't all fricasseed frogs and eel pie."
—THE SILVER CHAIR

1. Put the eel in a pot and cover with salted water. Soak for 1 hour. Rinse and cut the eel into 3" pieces.

2. In a sauté pan, heat the butter and cook the onion, carrots, and garlic until the onion is tender and translucent. Do not brown.

3. Season the eel with salt and pepper, and add to the pan, along with the bouquet garni and lemon peel. Pour in the wine and add enough water to cover the fish. Simmer, covered, for 30 minutes.

4. Remove the eel from the broth. Boil down the cooking broth to reduce by half. Strain the broth, and return both the broth and the pieces of eel to the pot. Reheat and serve sprinkled with parsley.

6 SERVINGS

2 pounds skinned and boned eel
2 tablespoons (¼ stick) butter
½ cup finely chopped onion
½ cup chopped carrots
1 clove garlic, finely chopped
Salt and pepper
1 bouquet garni (sprigs of fresh parsley and thyme tied together with a bay leaf)
Strip of lemon zest with no white pith attached
1 cup port wine
Chopped parsley

BOILED HAM

Now here is food fit for the finest banqueting tables of Cair Paravel or Buckingham Palace. If you can find someone who still makes hams in the old-fashioned way, you are very lucky. An autumn pig, peach fed and then cured and smoked, will produce the finest food ever devised. In Ireland they found out centuries ago that you can prepare a delicious ham by boiling it in a big pot for twenty minutes, taking the pot off the heat and wrapping it up in blankets or quilts to thoroughly insulate it, and leaving it overnight. If you have wrapped it up well enough, by the next morning it will be beautifully cooked and still too hot to touch. When you take it out, it is ready to be skinned and glazed. Sometimes I put a layer of fresh peach slices or plum halves on top of my hams before I glaze them. You can pin them to the ham with toothpicks.

From the roof—that is, from the underside
of the deck—hung hams and strings of onions, and also
the men of the watch off-duty in their hammocks.
—THE VOYAGE OF THE DAWN TREADER

15–18 SERVINGS

10–12 pound country
  smoked ham with bone
1 large onion
8 whole cloves
1 tablespoon sugar
4 bay leaves

1. If the ham has been aged and is quite dry and hard to the touch, soak in cold water for 24 hours. Most hams now are aged less and can be boiled immediately.

2. Place the ham in a large pot. Peel the onion, stud it with the cloves, and add it to the pot with the sugar and bay leaves and enough water to cover all. Bring to a simmer and cook 20 minutes per pound, or until the bone at the narrow end of the shank moves easily.

3. If the ham is to be baked and glazed, remove it from the liquid; cut away the thick skin, leaving a thin coating of fat; and then proceed to glaze and bake. To serve at room temperature unglazed or chilled, allow the ham to cool in the liquid, then remove and refrigerate.

To Glaze and Bake Ham:

1. Preheat the oven to 400 degrees F.

2. Score the fat of the hot ham with a knife into a diamond pattern. Stick a clove into the center of each diamond.

3. Combine the sugar, honey, mustard, and mace with enough orange juice to make a creamy mixture. Spread over the scored surface and sprinkle with bread crumbs.

4. Bake the ham for 30 minutes or until the glaze is set. Remove from the oven and allow to sit for 20 minutes before slicing.

Serve hot or cold ham with mustard and chutney.

Whole cloves
1 cup light-brown sugar
1/2 cup honey
2 tablespoons Dijon
   mustard
1/2 teaspoon mace
1/2-3/4 cup orange juice
1/2 cup dry bread crumbs
Mustard and chutney

◆

CHICKEN BREASTS MASQUERADING AS SNIPE

Snipe are a small migratory bird that used to be found all over Europe. Unfortunately for them, snipe are very delicious to eat, and as a result they are becoming quite scarce. They are not easy to shoot, however, as years of being hunted by men with shotguns have taught them to fly like maniacs and jink all over the sky. The word we use for a man who is an ace shot with a rifle, *sniper*, comes from the expertise needed to shoot these birds. We have substituted pieces of chicken in this recipe, because it is unlikely that you will be able to get snipe, or at least I hope so, as I think it is time we left the poor snipe alone. We have also left out the truffles, as you probably won't be able to find any of those either (unless, that is, you happen to live in the Périgord or Magny areas of France and have a pet pig trained as a truffle hunter). Truffles are wondrous edible fungi that grow quite deep underground, with no visible sign on the surface of their presence. Truffles are common in Narnia, and Badgers are renowned for serving them.

Clouds of birds were constantly alighting in them again—
duck, snipe, bitterns, herons.

—*THE SILVER CHAIR*

6 SERVINGS

6 boned chicken breast halves with skin. You can ask your butcher to prepare them this way if you cannot find them in the market.
1 tablespoon butter
3/4 cup finely chopped onion
3/4 cup chopped mushrooms
1/2 cup chopped almonds

1. Wash the chicken thoroughly, then carefully remove the skin from each portion of the chicken, keeping the skin in one piece. Reserve. Place the meat between sheets of plastic wrap, and with a mallet flatten each piece to a thin cutlet. Set aside the cutlets and skin.

2. Preheat the oven to 375 degrees F.

3. Melt the butter in a skillet and add the onion. Cook over low heat until tender and translucent. Do not brown. Add the mushrooms and cook 5 minutes. Remove all to a bowl.

4. Toast the almonds in the oven for 5 minutes.

Add to the vegetables. Mix in the bread crumbs, parsley, and thyme. Add the egg, and mix lightly until well combined.

5. Divide the stuffing among the chicken cutlets. Fold up the sides of the chicken around the stuffing and press in place. Place a piece of skin on top of each "bird" and tuck it around the meat to hold the stuffing inside. Secure with toothpicks. Brush each with a little oil, season with salt and pepper, and place in an oiled ovenproof pan.

6. Bake for 1 hour until cooked through and nicely browned. Remove toothpicks, and serve with pan juices.

2¹/₂ cups coarse fresh bread crumbs

1 tablespoon finely chopped fresh parsley

1 tablespoon finely chopped fresh thyme leaves, or 1 teaspoon dried

1 egg, beaten

Olive oil

1 tablespoon salt, plus a little extra

1 tablespoon freshly ground pepper, plus a little extra

◆

COLD POACHED SALMON

The Narnian fish pavender is found in both the sea and rivers of Narnia, and is a favorite of everybody, from Marsh-wiggles to kings and queens at Cair Paravel and Castle Anvard. The fish most like the pavender is the Atlantic salmon, found in the rivers of Scotland and Ireland, so we have used this fish for our recipe. The name *pavender* comes from a conversation that Jack was having with my mother and some friends at the Trout Inn, in Wolvercote, Oxfordshire. As you sit on the riverside terrace at the Trout, lots of fish will come and beg to be fed scraps from your lunch. Someone made a point of telling Jack that they are a fish called "chavender, or chubb," so when Jack wanted to name his Narnian fish, it seemed natural to call them "pavender, or pub."

> There were soups that would make your mouth water to think of, and the lovely fishes called pavenders.
> —THE SILVER CHAIR

6 SERVINGS

1 whole salmon, 4–5
   pounds, cleaned and
   scaled
4 sprigs fresh parsley
4 sprigs fresh dill
1 onion
½ lemon
6 peppercorns
1 bay leaf
2 teaspoons salt
1 cup dry white wine
Slices of lemon
Watercress
Herbed mayonnaise (see
   recipe opposite)

1. Choose a pot or roasting pan large enough to hold the salmon. Tuck the parsley and dill into the cavity of the fish. Place the fish in the pan. Peel and slice the onion; add to the pan. Squeeze lemon juice from the half lemon over the fish, and add the squeezed rind to the pan. Add the pepper, bay leaf, and salt.

2. Pour the wine over the fish, and add water to cover. Bring to a simmer, and cook 10 minutes per pound, or until the flesh is barely cooked.

3. Remove the fish from the poaching liquid, and allow to cool to room temperature. Cover with plastic wrap and chill until shortly before serving.

4. To serve, remove the skin from the fish. Garnish the top of the fish with slices of lemon and surround with watercress. Serve with herbed mayonnaise.

Herbed Mayonnaise

1. In a blender, combine the egg yolks, mustard, white pepper, and vinegar.

2. With the machine running, add the oils drop by drop at first, gradually adding them in a slow stream as the mixture thickens. Blend in the lemon juice.

3. Spoon mayonnaise into a bowl and add the herbs. Taste for seasoning and add as needed.

* When salmonella from raw eggs is a concern, substitute store-bought mayonnaise and simply add the chopped herbs.

2 egg yolks*
1 teaspoon dry mustard
¼ teaspoon white pepper
1 teaspoon tarragon
  vinegar
½ cup olive oil
½ cup canola oil
1 teaspoon lemon juice
1 tablespoon finely
  chopped fresh parsley
1 teaspoon finely chopped
  fresh chives
1 teaspoon finely chopped
  fresh dill

Ember-Roasted Salmon

This is another fine way to prepare fish (pavenders if you can get them, but in this world, salmon is the next best thing). Since the very beginning of time, all over our world and in Narnia, fish have been roasted in the glowing coals of open fires. You know what? It is still one of the best ways to cook fish.

But he cheered up when it came to lighting the fire and showing them how to roast the fresh pavenders in the embers.

—*Prince Caspian*

6 SERVINGS

2 sheets heavy-duty foil
2½ pound fillet of salmon, scaled
2 tablespoons (¼ stick) butter
2 tablespoons chopped fresh dill
Salt and white pepper
6 slices lemon
2 tablespoons dry white wine

1. Preheat a gas or charcoal grill.

2. Stack the foil sheets and place the salmon in the center. Dot the salmon with the butter and top with the dill; add salt and pepper. Arrange the lemon slices on the fish. Begin to wrap the foil up around the fish to partially seal it. Drizzle the wine over all. Seal all edges well.

3. Place on the gas or charcoal grill and cook about 15 minutes, turning over after 10 minutes. This will result in very rare salmon. Leave over the fire longer for well done.

The cooking time can be shortened to about 10 minutes by dividing the fish and other ingredients into 6 packets.

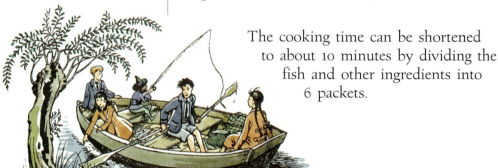

◆

FRESH FRIED FISH

You may remember the scene in *The Lion, the Witch and the Wardrobe* in which Mr. Beaver goes out to a hole in the ice and, with his paw, catches fish that Mrs. Beaver fries up for dinner. If you can build a campfire right beside a river or lake, catch your fish, clean them, cook them, and eat them, all within the same hour, you will have eaten fish at its very best. Narnia doesn't have our kind of modern technology, so food has to be eaten fresh through most of the year, just the same as it used to be in our world back in the Middle Ages.

> *You can think how good the new-caught fish*
> *smelled while they were frying.*
> —THE LION, THE WITCH AND THE WARDROBE

1. Rinse the fish and dry with paper towels.

2. Beat the eggs with a fork to mix. Slowly heat ½" oil in a heavy skillet. It will be necessary to use more than one skillet or to cook the fish in more than one batch.

3. Sprinkle the fish with salt and pat with flour. Dip the fish in the egg wash to coat, and slide gently into the hot oil. Fry until the first side is golden brown; then turn over and cook the other side. Cooking time is about 4 minutes per side.

4. Remove the fish from the pan and drain well on paper towels. Serve hot, garnished with chopped parsley and lemon wedges.

A batter coating (p. 64) may be used instead of the egg wash for a more substantial crust.

6 SERVINGS

6 whole brook trout, cleaned, about 8 ounces each
2 eggs
Oil for frying
2 teaspoons salt
4 tablespoons all-purpose flour
1 tablespoon fresh chopped parsley
6 lemon wedges

◆

1½ cups all-purpose flour
3 teaspoons baking
   powder
1 teaspoon salt
2 eggs
1 cup milk

Batter

1. Combine the flour, baking powder, and salt.

2. Beat the eggs until frothy. Stir the milk into the eggs.

3. Add the dry ingredients to the egg-milk mixture and beat until smooth.

4. Dip the flour-coated fillets into the batter and then fry as above.

◆

CHICKEN LIVERS CALORMENE

Calormen is an interesting country. Living in a climate that is much hotter than Narnia's, Calormenes can grow all kinds of interesting things that Narnians can't. Their country was founded long ago by outlaws, and, living in this harsh and difficult land, they developed into a cruel and hard civilization. However, the upper levels of their society, the Tarkaans and Tarkheenas, tend to be self-indulgent people, and their cooks have had to think up delicious foods to pamper their nobility. This chicken liver recipe is an example of their fine cooking.

"Now, princeling," he said.
"Make a good dinner. It will be
your last meal in Tashbaan."
—THE HORSE AND HIS BOY

1. Grease a baking sheet.

2. Drain the livers and blot dry with paper towels. The livers are first coated in the butter, then in the crumbs—the butter helps the crumbs stick to the livers. Sprinkle with salt and pepper. Arrange on the greased baking sheet and set aside.

3. To begin the sauce, melt the 2 tablespoons of butter in a small saucepan and stir in the onion powder, cayenne, mustard, ketchup, and Worcestershire sauce. Set aside.

4. In a sauté pan over medium heat, melt 1 tablespoon of butter and 1 tablespoon of olive oil. Add the onion and cook until soft and translucent. Do not brown. Stir in the rice to coat with the oil. Add the allspice and 1 cup of chicken broth.

6 SERVINGS

FOR THE CHICKEN
LIVERS:

1 pound chicken livers
3 tablespoons (3/8 stick)
butter, melted
2/3 cup fresh bread
crumbs, very fine
Salt and pepper

FOR THE SAUCE:

2 tablespoons (¼ stick)
   butter
½ teaspoon onion powder
Dash of cayenne
2 tablespoons Dijon
   mustard
1 tablespoon tomato
   ketchup
2 teaspoons
   Worcestershire sauce

FOR THE RICE:

1 tablespoon butter
1 tablespoon olive oil
1 onion, chopped, about
   1 cup
1 cup rice
1 teaspoon ground allspice
2–2½ cups chicken broth
¼ cup raisins
Salt and pepper
½ cup pignoli or almonds,
   toasted

Simmer 5 minutes, and add the raisins and more broth as the liquid is absorbed. After 18–20 minutes of cooking, the rice should be tender and moist but not soupy. Add salt and pepper to taste.

5. While the rice is cooking, preheat the broiler, and cook the chicken livers about 3 minutes on each side.

6. To finish the dish, heat the sauce over low heat. Spoon the rice around the edge of a warmed platter, and sprinkle with the nuts. Fill the center with the chicken livers and serve the sauce on the side.

BOILED POTATOES

Potatoes originated in America and were introduced to England and to Ireland during the reign of Elizabeth I; they soon became part of the staple diet of the people of both of these countries. There is no better food than the humble boiled spud, and you will find it on almost every table in Narnia.

Susan drained the potatoes and then put them all back in the empty pot to dry on the side of the range.
—*THE LION, THE WITCH AND THE WARDROBE*

1. Wash the potatoes and peel them; then put them in a pot and cover immediately with cold salted water, 1 teaspoon of salt per quart of water. If you leave the potatoes out in the air after they are peeled, they will turn brown.

6 SERVINGS

6 potatoes of uniform size

2. Bring the water to a boil, lower heat, and cook gently for about 15 minutes before testing with a skewer for doneness. Cook until just tender.

3. Drain the potatoes. If not serving immediately, return them to the pot. Cover the pot with a folded tea towel, and keep the pot in a warm place until it is time to serve the potatoes.

ROAST CHESTNUTS

In 1954 I was a little American boy sent off to an English boarding school; the best thing I learned in my entire seven years there was to roast and eat chestnuts. In winter in England you still see vendors with special wheeled braziers selling roasted chestnuts. They are delicious.

If you had been there you would probably have known (he didn't) that he was seeing oaks, beeches, silver birches, rowans, and sweet chestnuts.
—THE HORSE AND HIS BOY

Chestnuts
Butter

1. With a sharp knife make two slashes in a cross shape across the flat side of each nut, trying not to cut into the flesh of the nut.

2. Preheat the oven to 350 degrees F.

3. Melt about 1 teaspoon of butter for each cup of nuts. Toss the nuts in the butter to coat and arrange in 1 layer in a jelly roll pan.

4. Bake for about 30 minutes, until the nuts are tender and the shells can be removed easily.

If you are roasting nuts over an open fire, use a special chestnut roasting pan with a long handle. Slash the nuts as above, but do not use butter. Roast the nuts, shaking the pan constantly, until the meat of the nut can be pierced with the tip of a sharp knife. Cooking time will vary with the heat of the fire.

68

Homestyle Brown Bread

While fine white bread might often be served at Cair Paravel and Castle Anvard, the everyday bread used by most Narnians would be the more nutritious brown bread. Brown or white soda bread, as it's called in Ireland, is a very good food, and any Narnian cook knows how to make it very well. You will notice it doesn't contain any yeast, so it is very suitable for anyone with a yeast intolerance. It also tastes very good.

The very smell of the bread-and-milk he used to have for supper came back to him.
—The Last Battle

1. Preheat the oven to 425 degrees F. Grease two 8" x 4" x 2" loaf pans.

2. Stir together all dry ingredients.

3. Cut the butter into tiny cubes and add to the dry ingredients, rubbing them into the flour with your fingertips until the butter has disappeared.

4. Gradually stir in the buttermilk, using 1½ cups to start, adding more if necessary to make a fairly soft dough. (This will vary with the flour and humidity day to day.)

5. Turn the dough out on a lightly floured surface and knead a few times. Divide in two and form into loaves. Place loaves into prepared pans and bake for 30–35 minutes, until browned and cooked through. Internal temperature should read 190 degrees F when checked with an instant-read thermometer.

6. Turn out on a rack to cool completely before slicing.

2 LOAVES

3 cups all-purpose flour
1½ cups whole-wheat flour or American-Irish flour, available in specialty stores
½ cup rolled oats, not instant
⅓ cup steel-cut oats
2½ teaspoons baking soda
⅓ cup firmly packed light-brown sugar
4 tablespoons (½ stick) butter, room temperature
1½ cups buttermilk, plus more if needed

ROAST POTATOES

Another thing I learned at boarding school was that if you wrap a potato in a layer of wet clay and toss it into the glowing coals of a campfire, after about forty minutes, when you take it out and crack off the clay, the potato inside will be deliciously cooked. Some people don't even bother with the clay but just chuck the potato straight into the coals. This results in a thin layer of black crust around the potato, and that, too, is delicious. Roast potatoes go very well with roast meat, and this way you can cook both the meat and the potatoes in the same oven all at the same time. Narnians, especially Dwarfs, love potatoes and always put some in with anything they are roasting.

And great mugs of frothy chocolate, and roast potatoes and roast chestnuts, and baked apples with raisins stuck in where the cores had been, and then ices just to freshen you up after all the hot things.
—THE SILVER CHAIR

6 SERVINGS

6 potatoes of uniform size
2 tablespoons olive oil
1 tablespoon finely
  chopped garlic
1 tablespoon chopped
  fresh rosemary
Salt and freshly ground
  black pepper

1. Preheat the oven to 400 degrees F.

2. Scrub the potatoes well and cut out any spots. You may peel them or leave the peel on as desired.

3. In a shallow ovenproof pan large enough to hold the potatoes in one layer, mix together the oil, garlic, and rosemary. Roll the potatoes in the oil to coat, and season with salt and pepper.

4. Cover the pan tightly with foil and roast the potatoes for 30 minutes. At this point they should be firm but pierced easily with a sharp knife. Cooking time will vary with the size of the potatoes. When barely tender, remove the foil and return to the oven to brown, about 15 minutes more.

Potatoes can also be roasted in an open fire. Wash and prepare as above. Roll in herbed oil and wrap each one in a square of heavy-duty foil. Place the packets in the coals, spreading some embers on top. Turn the packets every 15 minutes or so. Cooking time will vary with the size of the potatoes and the heat of the fire. Test by poking a skewer into a potato after about 40 minutes.

SAUSAGE

Sausages and sausage meat were invented in order to use the various little bits of meat that are too small to be used for anything else. In Narnia, folks deplore waste, and so for centuries they have been great makers of sausages. There is a fine art to making good sausages, and every good butcher has his own secret mixture of herbs and spices. This is a good, basic recipe.

She had a vague impression of Dwarfs crowding round the fire with frying pans rather bigger than themselves, and the hissing, and delicious smell of sausages, and more, and more, and more sausages.
—THE SILVER CHAIR

ABOUT 2 POUNDS, 8–10 PATTIES

1½ pounds lean pork, cubed and very cold
⅓–½ pound pork fat, cubed and very cold
1 teaspoon salt
½ teaspoon ground allspice
½ teaspoon freshly ground black pepper
1 teaspoon ground dried sage
½ cup dried bread crumbs, very fine

1. In the bowl of a food processor, chop ¼ of the meat and ¼ of the fat together. Use more or less fat depending upon the leanness of the meat. The ratio of meat to fat should be about 4 to 1. As each portion is chopped, place in a mixing bowl.

2. Mix in the salt, allspice, pepper, sage, and bread crumbs by hand. Make a small patty of about a tablespoon of the mixture; fry it slowly in a small pan and taste for seasoning, then add more seasoning to the uncooked mixture if needed. Do not taste the uncooked meat.

3. Form the meat into sausage shapes or patties. In a lightly greased heavy frying pan, cook the sausage slowly until browned on all sides and cooked thoroughly.

Sausage Rolls

1. Bring the pastry to room temperature. Divide it into 3 pieces and roll out slightly.

2. Preheat the oven to 400 degrees F.

3. Divide the sausage into 3 portions and form a long cylinder of meat down the length of each sheet of pastry.

4. Paint the edges of each piece of pastry with the egg wash and seal, pressing firmly to make a long roll.

5. Place the rolls on an ungreased cookie sheet. Cut almost through each roll to make 4 large or 12 bite-size portions.

6. Bake until the pastry is browned and the sausage is cooked, about 20 minutes. Allow to cool slightly before serving.

36 BITE-SIZE OR 12 LARGE PIECES

½ package purchased frozen puff pastry (about ½ pound)
½ pound uncooked sausage meat
1 egg beaten with 1 tablespoon water

◆

DESSERT

In Roman times, long before Narnia was created, enormous
expense and care went into the preparation of hundreds of different kinds of desserts. Down through the ages of English and
Narnian history, chefs and cooks would take great pride in their
skill and artistry in preparing desserts that not only tasted wonderful but were great pieces of visual art as well. Even today most
chefs like to make their desserts the crowning glory of the dinner. Dessert recipes nowadays use a wide variety of materials and
flavors and are often very rich. What you serve for dessert should
depend on what you have had in the preceding courses—a light
dessert is nice after a rich main course, and a rich, heavier dessert
goes well following a light main course. You can have a lot of fun
with desserts by using your own skill and imagination. In Narnia
desserts tend to be richer in the winter. Also, just as in this world,
winter is a time for hot desserts and puddings rather than cold
ones. The final touch to the dessert course is usually some kind
of candy or sweet fruit.

LUCY'S ROAST APPLES

There are several ways of baking apples, both here and in Narnia, and this is one of the very best. A nice, sweet baked apple is a really excellent dessert on a cold winter's night. If you want to be really posh, just before you serve the baked apple, pour a little applejack, if you can get it, or fine brandy over the apple and get a responsible adult to set it on fire. The alcohol will burn off, leaving a rich flavor behind. It looks very dramatic and tastes good too.

They tried roasting some of the apples on the ends of sticks.

—PRINCE CASPIAN

6 SERVINGS

6 firm apples; Granny
  Smiths are the best to
  use; Rome or McIntosh
  are good too.
6 tablespoons brown sugar
6 tablespoons raisins
¼ teaspoon cinnamon
Sweetened whipped cream
  or vanilla ice cream,
  optional

1. Preheat the oven to 375 degrees F. Grease a baking dish large enough to hold the apples.

2. Wash the apples and remove the cores without breaking through the bottom. Place the apples in the baking dish.

3. Combine the sugar, raisins, and cinnamon and pack into cavities. Pile any extra filling on top. Pour boiling water around the apples to a depth of ¼". Cover and bake for 45 minutes or until the apples are tender but still hold their shape.

4. Remove the apples to a serving dish and boil the juices in the pan until slightly thickened. Pour over the apples.

5. Serve apples warm or chilled, topping with whipped cream or ice cream, if desired.

76

SWEETMEATS

There are many different kinds of sweetmeats, and the word really refers to what the English call sweets and the Americans call candy. The making of sweetmeats is an art in itself, and the Calormene people have long been specialists in this field. Here are a couple of fairly simple recipes.

It was much more crowded than Shasta had expected: crowded partly by the peasants (on their way to market) who had come in with them, but also with water sellers, sweetmeat sellers, porters, soldiers, beggars, ragged children, hens, stray dogs, and barefooted slaves.

—THE HORSE AND HIS BOY

Chocolate-Covered Hazelnuts

ABOUT 25 PIECES

2 cups hazelnuts, shelled
½ pound semisweet chocolate

1. Toast the nuts in a 350 degree F oven for 10 minutes. Remove them to a tea towel and rub to remove as much skin as possible.

2. Break the chocolate into small pieces and melt them in the top of a double boiler over simmering water. When completely melted, remove from heat and stir in the nuts.

3. Using a tablespoon, drop portions of the mixture onto the parchment paper and allow to cool. Store in a cool place.

These can be made with raisins or with peanuts or walnuts, either whole or chopped.

1 cup golden raisins
8 ounces dried apricots
½ teaspoon vanilla extract
½ teaspoon orange extract
1 cup shredded coconut,
*   either sweetened or*
*   unsweetened*

Fruit Truffles

1. Chop raisins very fine in a food processor. Add the apricots and process until quite well ground. Add the extracts.

2. Place the coconut on wax paper or a plate. Scoop out the fruit mixture a teaspoonful at a time and roll in the coconut. Roll each ball firmly between your hands. Spread a little coconut on a tray and arrange the truffles in one layer, scattering any extra coconut in between and over the sweets. Wrap airtight until ready to serve.

MARMALADE ROLL

This is a lovely dessert (called a pudding in England) for a cold winter's day, though of course you can eat it at any time, and it is a great favorite of the Dwarf folk. The Calormenes grow oranges, so they are available in Narnia for marmalade, but you can use other preserves, like strawberry jam, just to vary the flavor. This is very nice when served with a sweet cornstarch sauce or with custard.

And when they had finished the fish, Mrs. Beaver brought unexpectedly out of the oven a great and gloriously sticky marmalade roll.
—The Lion, the Witch and the Wardrobe

1. Line a 10" x 15" x 1" jelly roll pan with buttered parchment paper. Spread out a tea towel and sprinkle it with confectioners' sugar. Preheat the oven to 425 degrees F.

2. Sift together the cake flour, baking powder, and salt.

3. Using an electric mixer, beat the eggs until they thicken slightly and become lemon colored. Continue to beat while adding the water and the sugar.

6–8 SERVINGS

Confectioners' sugar
1 cup cake flour, sifted before measuring
2 teaspoons baking powder
1/4 teaspoon salt
3 large eggs
1/4 cup cold water
1 cup granulated sugar
1 teaspoon vanilla
1/2 cup orange marmalade

4. With a spatula, fold the dry ingredients into the egg mixture until they disappear. Stir in the vanilla.

5. Pour into the prepared pan, spreading to the edges. Bake 10–12 minutes, checking for doneness after 10 minutes. The top of the cake should be light golden brown and firm to the touch. Remove from the oven.

6. Invert the cake on the tea towel and carefully remove the paper. Immediately spread all but 2 tablespoons of the marmalade evenly over the surface of the hot cake. Starting with a long edge and using the tea towel as a help, roll the cake into a log. It may crack slightly. Spread the reserved marmalade over the top of the cake and sprinkle with a little confectioners' sugar. Allow the cake to cool before cutting.

STEAMED PUDDING AND GINGER FIG PUDDING

Two Narnian favorites. I first encountered steamed pudding at boarding school and have loved it ever since. It's really delicious served with maple syrup, golden syrup (cane syrup), or a custard sauce. You can add chocolate to the mixture and make a chocolate steamed pudding, which can be served with a sweet white cornstarch sauce. The plain steamed pudding is especially good with a sweet chocolate cornstarch sauce. These puddings are hearty, filling, and very scrumptious.

Edmund couldn't quite see what they were eating, but it smelled lovely and there seemed to be decorations of holly and he wasn't at all sure that he didn't see something like a plum pudding.
—THE LION, THE WITCH AND THE WARDROBE

Steamed Pudding

6 SERVINGS

1. Butter a 1-quart pudding basin or heatproof bowl, and butter a piece of parchment paper big enough to cover the bowl.

2. By hand or with an electric mixer, beat the butter until creamy. Beat in the sugar until the mixture is smooth.

3. Mix the flour and salt together, and add it to the butter and sugar alternately with the beaten eggs.

4. Stir the vanilla into the milk and mix into the pudding.

5. Spoon the pudding into the prepared bowl or basin, and cover with the buttered parchment paper and then with foil, securing with a string.

4 tablespoons (½ stick) butter
½ cup granulated sugar
½ cup self-rising flour
Pinch of salt
2 large eggs, beaten
½ teaspoon vanilla extract
2 tablespoons milk
    Sauce or topping as desired (p. 83)

81

6. Steam the pudding in a steamer or on a saucer above simmering water in large covered saucepan for 1½ hours, adding more water to the pan as necessary.

7. Remove the pudding basin from the pan of hot water and cool for 10 minutes. Uncover the pudding; invert the basin over a serving platter and shake or tap the basin to unmold. Serve warm with desired sauce.

Ginger Fig Pudding

6–8 SERVINGS

½ pound dried figs
1 large egg
1 cup molasses
8 tablespoons (1 stick) butter, melted
1 teaspoon baking soda
2½ cups flour
1 teaspoon salt
1 tablespoon ground ginger
3/4 cup water from soaking figs
2 tablespoons finely chopped preserved ginger
Sauce or topping as desired (see recipe opposite)

1. Butter a 1½-quart pudding basin or heatproof bowl and a piece of parchment paper big enough to cover the top of the bowl.

2. Place the figs in a small bowl and add boiling water to cover. Soak for 10 minutes. Drain, reserving 3/4 cup of water. Clip off the stems and chop figs finely.

3. In a large bowl, beat the egg and stir in the molasses, melted butter, and baking soda.

4. Sift the flour, salt, and ground ginger, and add to the egg mixture alternately with the water. Stir in the figs and the preserved ginger.

5. Spoon the pudding into the prepared bowl; cover with the buttered parchment paper and foil and secure with a string.

6. Steam the pudding in a steamer or on a saucer above simmering water in a large covered saucepan for 2½ hours, adding additional water to the pan as necessary.

7. Unmold as in previous recipe.

Appropriate toppings for puddings include golden syrup, custard sauce, warmed jam, lightly sweetened whipped cream, or hard sauce.

◆

Custard Sauce

ABOUT 2 CUPS

2 cups milk
1 tablespoon cornstarch
2 large eggs
2 tablespoons granulated
  sugar
1 teaspoon vanilla extract

1. Pour about 2 tablespoons of the milk into a small bowl and stir in the cornstarch to dissolve.

2. In a small saucepan, beat the eggs and the remaining milk with the sugar; then cook over medium heat, stirring constantly, until the mixture begins to bubble around the edges.

3. Stir in the dissolved cornstarch and continue to cook for 1 or 2 minutes as the custard thickens. Remove from heat.

4. Stir in the vanilla. If not using immediately, cover the surface of the custard with plastic wrap to prevent a skin from forming.

Custard sauce may be served warm or cold. It becomes thicker when chilled.

Hard Sauce

ABOUT $^3/_4$ CUP

5 tablespoons butter, room
  temperature
1 cup confectioners' sugar
1 tablespoon boiling water
$^1/_2$ teaspoon vanilla extract

Using a mixer or by hand, cream the butter and sugar together, and mix in the water and the vanilla until smooth. Serve at room temperature.

Variation: Substitute 2 teaspoons grated orange rind and 1 tablespoon orange juice for the water and vanilla.

Mincemeat Pies

Often just called mince pies, they are a traditional Christmas dessert in England. They are very rich and filling, and most children love them. I first encountered them during Christmas at The Kilns. They are often found on fine tables in Narnia.

For a heavenly smell, warm and golden, as if from all the most delicious fruits and flowers of the world, was coming up to them from somewhere ahead.

—The Magician's Nephew

EIGHTEEN 2½" PIES, PLUS
1 FREE-FORM TART

12 tablespoons (1½ sticks)
 butter
2½ cups all-purpose flour
Pinch of salt
2 tablespoons granulated
 sugar
2 egg yolks beaten with 2
 tablespoons water
2 cups commercially pre-
 pared mincemeat, such
 as Cross & Blackwell
1 tart apple, peeled and
 chopped
Milk, for brushing the
 pastry
Superfine sugar

1. Cut the butter into 12 pieces and chill in the freezer for 10 minutes.

2. Combine the flour, salt, and sugar.

3. With a pastry cutter or a knife, cut the pieces of butter into the flour until the mixture resembles coarse meal.

4. Using a fork, mix in the egg yolks. Gradually add more water as needed to form workable dough—3–5 tablespoons. Working the dough as little as possible, form it into a disk. Wrap in plastic wrap and refrigerate 1 hour or until ready to use.

5. Grease 2 patty pans (nine 2½" cups) or a cookie sheet. Patty pans are available in cookware specialty stores. Preheat the oven to 400 degrees F.

6. Combine the mincemeat and apple. Divide the pastry into 2 portions. Refrigerate 1 portion while working with the first. Roll the pastry very thin, about ⅛" thick. Cut out as many 3" rounds as you can. Place half in the patty pans or on the cookie sheet. Spoon 1 tablespoon of filling in the center of each round. Brush the edges with water; top with the remaining rounds of pastry, and press each

with the tines of a fork to seal the edges well.
Repeat with the second portion of the pastry.
Brush each pie top lightly with milk; prick each
pie top with a skewer to allow steam to escape
and bake for 15–20 minutes, or until the tops are
golden.

7. Remove from the pans to a cooling rack and
sprinkle with superfine sugar.

8. Roll pastry scraps into a thin round; spread the
center with the leftover filling. Fold the edges in to
almost meet in the center. Brush the pastry with
milk. Place on a greased baking sheet and bake
until golden, about 30 minutes.

◆

Tea Cakes with Lemon Curd Filling

Here is another delicious dessert that is also very good for you, as it is rich in vitamin C. Lemon curd is also very nice on fresh bread and butter as a sweet sandwich. Narnians preparing this dessert will have to get their lemons from the Calormene traders because lemons don't grow in Narnia.

"Daughter of Eve from the far land of Spare Oom where eternal summer reigns around the bright city of War Drobe, how would it be if you came and had tea with me?"
—THE LION, THE WITCH AND THE WARDROBE

12 SERVINGS

4 tablespoons (½ stick)
  butter, at room
  temperature
½ cup granulated sugar
⅔ cup all-purpose flour
1 teaspoon baking powder
Pinch of salt
1 large egg
⅔ cup milk
½ teaspoon vanilla extract,
  or grated zest of ½
  lemon
Lemon curd (see recipe
  opposite)
Confectioners' sugar

1. Line a 12-cup muffin pan with paper liners. Spray with a nonstick cooking spray. Preheat the oven to 350 degrees F.

2. Using an electric mixer, beat the butter and granulated sugar until fluffy.

3. Sift together the flour, baking powder, and salt.

4. Beat the egg and combine with the milk and vanilla or lemon zest.

5. Add the dry ingredients and milk mixture to the butter and sugar in alternate batches, mixing well after each addition.

6. Fill the paper liners halfway with batter and bake for 20 minutes, or until the centers are firm and the edges begin to color. Remove to a rack to cool.

7. When the cakes are completely cool, remove from the muffin pan and, using a melon baller or a sharp knife, scoop a sphere out of the top of each cake. Spoon a dollop of lemon curd into the hole and replace the top. Sift confectioners' sugar over the cakes.

Lemon Curd Filling

2 CUPS

2 large lemons
8 tablespoons (1 stick) butter
1 cup granulated sugar
2 large eggs

1. Wash the lemons. Grate the zest first and then squeeze the juice from the lemons, about ½ cup. Strain out the pits.

2. Place the grated zest, ¼ cup of the lemon juice, the butter, and the sugar in the top of a double boiler over boiling water. Stir until the butter is melted and the sugar is dissolved. Cook about 10 minutes more. Set aside while beating the eggs.

3. Beat the eggs until light and frothy, and add the remaining lemon juice. Very gradually beat in about 1/2 the sugar mixture. The mixture will still be hot, so you must beat it into the eggs *very* gradually. Then return all to the double boiler and cook, stirring, until the curd has thickened.

4. Pour the lemon curd into a sterilized* 1 pint jelly jar. Cool and store in the refrigerator.

*To sterilize a jelly jar, put it on a rack in a large saucepan. The cover of the jar may be sterilized at the same time. Add water to cover. Bring the water to a boil, and then simmer 10 minutes. Leave the jar in the water until ready to fill, then remove with tongs, drain, and fill.

◆

GOOSEBERRY FOOL

The real mystery about gooseberry fool is why it is called fool. I think it probably comes from the French word *fouler* which means "to crush, squash, or trample," which is very appropriate because you do have to squash up your gooseberries, rhubarb, or other fruit into a puree to make a fool. Rich and delicious, this is a very good summer treat. Dryads and Naiads are particularly fond of this attractive dessert.

There were cool melons and gooseberry fools and mulberry fools, and every kind of nice thing that can be made with ice.
—THE HORSE AND HIS BOY

6 SERVINGS

1 pound gooseberries, or a
  2-pound jar cooked
  gooseberries
½ cup granulated sugar
3/4 cup water
3/4 cup heavy cream
Sprigs of fresh mint

1. If using fresh berries, cook with the sugar and water until tender, about 10 minutes. Allow to cool.

2. Drain the cooked berries, either fresh or from a jar, and puree. Strain through fine mesh. You will have about 1¼ cups of puree.

3. In a separate cool bowl, whip the cream to soft peaks and combine with the cooled puree. Taste and add additional sugar if needed. Serve garnished with sprigs of mint.

Variation: Strawberries, raspberries, and blackberries may also be used. These do not need to be cooked; simply puree the berries, strain, and combine the puree with an equal amount of whipped cream and sugar to taste.

Rhubarb Fool

1. Remove the root ends from the rhubarb and wash. Cut into 1" pieces.

2. Place the rhubarb in a saucepan with the water and sugar; bring to a boil, and then lower heat and simmer until tender, about 10 minutes. Remove from heat and allow to cool completely.

3. In a separate cool bowl, whip the cream to soft peaks and combine with cooled fruit. Serve garnished with a sprinkle of cinnamon.

6 SERVINGS

1½ pound rhubarb, with
   no leaves attached
½ cup water
1 cup sugar
1 cup heavy cream
Ground cinnamon

TOFFEE

Toffee has been a favorite candy of English schoolchildren for longer than anyone can remember. There are lots of different kinds, but the toffee Digory planted in Narnia and which grew into a toffee tree is the sort you can still buy today all over England. When you find yourself on a journey through the wilds of Narnia and you don't have any food, a bag of good toffee will keep you going for a long time. You might even find a toffee tree.

"Wake up, Digory, wake up, Fledge," came the voice of Polly.
"It has turned into a toffee tree."
—THE MAGICIAN'S NEPHEW

ABOUT 2 POUNDS

1 cup granulated sugar
3/4 cup dark corn syrup
8 tablespoons (1 stick)
  butter, melted
1 cup evaporated milk
1 teaspoon vanilla

1. Butter a 9" square pan.

2. In a 5–6 quart saucepan, combine the sugar, syrup, butter, and milk. Bring to a boil over medium heat, stirring constantly. Continue to cook, lowering heat if the mixture starts to boil over. Cook until the mixture reaches 330 degrees F on a candy thermometer. Remove from heat and stir in the vanilla. Pour into the 9" square pan.

3. Cool in the pan for 20 minutes. Cut into squares and wrap each piece in parchment paper.

STRAWBERRY ICE CREAM

The term *ices* was used back in the Victorian era to mean ice cream, while frozen desserts made without milk or cream were called water ices. This recipe works with milk or water. Ice cream has become popular all over the world both as a dessert and sweet snack enjoyed any time of the day. In Narnia ices are a special treat and are served only as desserts for fine dinners and banquets. *Ices* when referring to food always means "ice cream" in Narnia.

And one tried very hard not to think of drinks—iced sherbet in a palace at Tashbaan, clear spring water tinkling with a dark earthy sound, cold smooth milk just creamy enough and not too creamy.
—THE HORSE AND HIS BOY

1. Beat the egg yolks with the sugar and the salt until the sugar is dissolved. Stir in the half and half.

1½ QUARTS

4 yolks from large eggs
½ cup granulated sugar
Pinch of salt
2 cups half and half
1 cup heavy cream, chilled
1 teaspoon vanilla extract
1 pint strawberries, pureed and chilled (about 1½ cups puree)

91

2. Transfer the mixture to a saucepan and cook over medium heat, stirring constantly, until it just begins to boil. It will thicken slightly. Remove from heat immediately and continue to stir for a minute or two.

3. Strain the custard into a bowl and chill completely.

4. Combine the chilled custard, heavy cream, vanilla, and strawberry puree in the can of an electric ice cream freezer and freeze, following the manufacturer's direcitons. Freezing time will vary from 25 to 50 minutes, depending upon the temperature of the mixture and the ratio of ice and salt in the freezer. When the mixture is completely frozen, unplug the freezer and remove the can of ice cream. Lift out the paddle.

5. If the ice cream is not to be served immediately, stir it and pack it down in the can. Cover the top with plastic wrap and the lid and store in the freezer.

◆

JELLY

What they call jelly in England and Narnia is what is called Jell-O in America. It's fun to make your own jellies using a variety of different fruits to flavor them. Jelly is a very old dessert and and is a nutritious food, as gelatin is almost pure protein. It is obtained from the hooves of cattle and pigs; the very best gelatin comes from calves' feet. There is also a kind of jelly made from seaweed, which is popular in Southeast Asia. Traditionally, in both Narnia and our world, well-made, good jellies are left to set in decorative molds so that when you serve them they arrive at the table in beautiful sculpted shapes. Jelly is a light dessert, excellent for summer dinners, and a favorite of the Naiads.

But when at last they were both seated after a meal (it was chiefly of the whipped cream and jelly and fruit and ice sort) in a beautiful pillared room (which Aravis would have liked better if Lasaraleen's spoiled pet monkey hadn't been climbing about all the time) Lasaraleen at last askd her why she was running away from home.

—THE HORSE AND HIS BOY

Lemon Jelly

1. Stir the gelatin into ½ cup of water to soften, about 5 minutes.

2. In a small saucepan, combine the remaining water with the lemon juice and sugar, and bring to a boil, stirring until the sugar is dissolved.

3. Remove the sugar mixture from heat and stir in the dissolved gelatin until well combined. Add grated lemon zest.

4. Rinse a 4-cup mold with cold water and shake out. The mold should be wet but not have any extra water in it. Pour in the jelly and refrigerate until set, 2 to 4 hours depending on the mold. Metal molds will jell faster; ceramic molds take longer.

4 SERVINGS

1 envelope unflavored
   gelatin
1½ cups water
½ cup lemon juice
½ cup granulated sugar
Grated zest of 1 lemon

93

5. To unmold, warm the outside of the mold for 10–15 seconds using a hot, wet towel or by lowering the mold into a basin of very warm water. Place a plate upside down over the top of the mold, invert the plate, and shake or rap the bottom of the mold.

Variation: Other flavored jellies may be made with favorite juices, such as orange juice, sweetening juices to taste and using 1 envelope of gelatin for every two cups of liquid.

Apple Jelly

4 SERVINGS

Juice and julienned rind of 1 lemon
1 pound apples, preferably McIntosh, peeled and sliced
1¼ cups water
6 tablespoons granulated sugar, or to taste
1 envelope unflavored gelatin

1. Peel the lemon and cut into julienne strips; then squeeze the juice.

2. Stew the apples with 1 cup of water, the sugar, lemon juice, and rind until the apples are very tender. Do not drain.

3. Press the apple mixture through a fine metal strainer and return the puree to the saucepan.

4. In a separate bowl, soften the gelatin in ¼ cup of water. Reheat the apple puree and stir in the softened gelatin until dissolved. Pour into a 2-cup mold, rinsed as in basic jelly recipe, and refrigerate until set.

◆

Mixed Fruit Jelly

1. Drain the fruit, reserving the juice. Measure the juice and add enough orange juice to measure 1½ cups.

2. In a separate bowl, soften the gelatin in the water.

3. In a saucepan, bring the juice to a boil; stir in the gelatin until dissolved. Remove from heat and mix in the fruit. Allow to cool to room temperature in the saucepan, stirring to distribute the fruit evenly, and then pour into the mold, rinsed as in basic jelly recipe.

4. Refrigerate until set, about 3–4 hours.

6 SERVINGS

One 3-ounce can fruit
  cocktail
Orange juice as needed to
  measure 1½ cups liquid
1 envelope unflavored
  gelatin
¼ cup water

CURDS

Curds and whey has always been a favorite among people who keep cows. The nursery rhyme "Little Miss Muffet" brings this to mind, as she sat "eating her curds and whey" (the curd is the solid part and the whey is the liquid). There are several ways of making curds. One method uses rennet, which is available in packets in many countries. Rennet is used to make a dessert called junket, a sweet curd usually flavored with vanilla or fruit juices and sugar. The curd described in this recipe is the kind found in Narnia. In Italy and Greece, milk is sometimes curdled by using the sap of a twig from a fig tree. The acids in citrus juices also cause milk to curdle. This recipe makes the favorite dessert of many Narnian children, whether they be Human, Faun, Dwarf, Centaur, Naiad or Dryad.

> . . . and gooseberries, redcurrants, curds, cream, milk, and mead.
> —THE VOYAGE OF THE DAWN TREADER

4 SERVINGS, ½ CUP EACH

1 tablet rennet, available under the Junket label in the pudding section of your market
1 tablespoon cold water
1½ cups whole milk
½ cup heavy cream
¼ cup honey

1. Set out 4 dessert bowls.

2. In a separate small bowl, crush the rennet tablet into a powder with the back of a spoon and dissolve it in the water.

3. In a saucepan, combine the milk, cream, and honey.

4. Over low heat, warm the milk mixture to lukewarm (110 degrees F). Remove from heat, add the rennet, and stir for 5–10 seconds. Pour into dessert bowls.

5. Let the dessert stand for 10–15 minutes before moving to the refrigerator to chill completely, about 2 hours.

TURKISH DELIGHT

Turkish delight is an ancient sweet from the Arabic nations of the world, where it is called *rahat lokhoum*, which means "perfumed sweetness." It was introduced to England by the explorer, writer, and adventurer Sir Richard Burton. It soon became a special treat at Christmas time and a part of the Christmas tradition. The White Witch used it to ensorcell Edmund because she wanted to make him her slave. Natural Turkish delight (not magical) is also a Christmas treat in Narnia. It should be eaten fresh and in small quantities, as it is very rich. Small children (whether Dwarf, Human, Faun, or Centaur) should be supervised when they are eating it, as it is so delicious they may just keep eating till it's all gone, which is the temptation.

He had eaten his share of the dinner, but he hadn't really enjoyed it because he was thinking all the time about Turkish Delight.
—THE LION, THE WITCH AND THE WARDROBE

ABOUT 1½ POUNDS

3 envelopes unflavored
  gelatin
½ cup cold water
½ cup hot water
2½ cups granulated sugar
¼ teaspoon salt
3 tablespoons lemon juice
½ teaspoon lemon extract
About ½ cup confection-
  ers' sugar, sifted

1. Soften the gelatin in the cold water. Set aside.

2. In a saucepan, bring the hot water and granulated sugar to a boil, stirring all the while. Lower heat. Add the salt, and stir in the softened gelatin until completely dissolved. Cook at a simmer for 20 minutes.

3. Remove from heat and let cool for 10 minutes. Stir in the lemon juice and lemon extract.

4. Rinse a 6" square pan with cold water. The pan should be wet but not have standing water. (A plastic sandwich box works well.) Pour the mixture into the pan. Cover with the box lid or plastic wrap and allow to stand in a cool place overnight.

5. Sift some of the confectioners' sugar onto a plate. Moisten a knife in very hot water and run it around the edges of the pan to loosen the candy. Invert the pan over the plate. It may be necessary to work on the edges a little to loosen them enough to turn the candy out on top of the sugar. Cut the square into equal-width strips. Roll each strip in sugar; then cut into cubes. Roll each cube in additional sugar to coat well.

A DISPLAY OF FRESH FRUIT

I feel fresh fruit is really the best way to end a meal. It looks nice, tastes good, and is good for you. What you put in your display of fresh fruit will depend on the season and where you live, though nowadays in America and England we are very lucky to be able to get all kinds of fruits from all over the world at almost any time. Some varieties have been bred for looks and nothing else, and as a result they have almost no flavor. On the other hand, some of the ugliest-looking fruits taste absolutely superb. Narnian fruits are all very rich in flavor, because Narnians care more for reality than for illusion.

> . . . *peaches, nectarines, pomegranates, pears, grapes, strawberries, raspberries—pyramids and cataracts of fruit.*
>
> —PRINCE CASPIAN

A display of fruit can be constructed for a few people or a large party. It can be designed with whole fruit, which will stay fresh over a good period of time, or with bite-size portions. Any unpeeled fruit should be washed carefully before using.

In a bowl or on a platter, group polished apples with a bunch of bananas and small bunches of grapes. Add tangerines or clementines for color and a different taste.

For a party, the fruit should be cut into portions that can be picked up easily or speared with toothpicks. Arrange the fruits in clusters on a large tray or platter and add mint sprigs or lemon leaves as a garnish. Add a little container of 3" skewers or decorative party toothpicks to the presentation.

USE ANY OF THE FRUITS MENTIONED ABOVE OR OTHER SEASONAL FRESH FRUITS AVAILABLE TO YOU, SUCH AS:

A variety of melons
Pineapples, kiwis, mangoes, bananas, apples
Oranges, tangerines, clementines

FOR GARNISH:

Grape or lemon leaves
Sprigs of mint

DRINKS

rinks are a very important part of everyone's diet. Everybody needs water. Over the centuries people have discovered all sorts of ways of adding flavor and also nutrition to water, which is, after all, the basis of all drinks. Today in this world we have all sorts of flavored drinks (my favorite is Dr Pepper), but in Narnia only natural ingredients and materials are used. Even so, their flavored drinks are absolutely delicious. Here are a few recipes to try.

Hot Chocolate

All who travel the oceans of Narnia or of this world beneath the tall masts and spreading canvas of sailing vessels find nothing more welcome during cold night watches than a large mug of hot chocolate. Cocoa, as it is called, has become a traditional drink in many great navies, both Narnian and Earthly. A tall ship, a star to steer her by, and a mug of hot cocoa. Who could ask for more?

"Perhaps something hot to drink?" said the Queen.
—*The Lion, the Witch and the Wardrobe*

PER SERVING:

1 tablespoon Dutch process unsweetened cocoa powder
1 heaping tablespoon granulated sugar (or sugar substitute to taste)
2 tablespoons cold water
1¼ cup milk
Sweetened whipped cream or a large marshmallow (optional)

1. Mix the cocoa powder and sugar with the water until dissolved.

2. In a small saucepan over medium heat, bring the milk to a boil. As it begins to boil, whisk in the cocoa mixture. Keep whisking as the cocoa froths up. Lift the pot off the heat as it rises to prevent the cocoa from boiling over. Pour into a mug and top with whipped cream or a marshmallow if desired.

IN PLACE OF MEAD

Mead is an alcoholic drink made out of honey, and was the traditional banqueting beverage of the Saxon warlords in the days of King Harold and before. While some people like it, it actually does not taste very nice, so we have substituted a couple of honey drinks that are very tasty. You can also put a large teaspoon of honey into a cup of boiling milk and have a nutritious and delicious drink to take to bed. Narnians make mead from wild honey, and Fauns and Dwarfs are quite partial to it.

The others liked the mead but Eustace was sorry afterward that he had drunk any.
—THE VOYAGE OF THE DAWN TREADER

Squeeze the lemon. You will have about 3 tablespoons of juice. Mix with the honey and pour into a glass. This may also be poured over ice in a tall glass and mixed with a little sparkling water.

PER PERSON:

1 lemon
1 tablespoon wildflower honey

Milk and Honey

Heat the milk until it just begins to bubble around the edges. Pour into a mug and stir in honey to taste.

PER PERSON:

1 cup milk
1 or 2 teaspoons wildflower honey

◆

Lemon Squash

This is a great drink on a hot day and, in fact, was the origin of all soft drinks. Strangely, in ancient times lemons, being very sour, were not considered edible at all. In the Roman Empire they were thought to be useful only as a medicine to combat the effect of poisonous snakes and insects. I suppose the lemon did not really come into its own until people began to think of mixing it with either honey or sugar to cut its acid sourness. Lemons do have a very advantageous soothing effect on sore throats and are still used as a medicinal fruit by the Naiad and Dryad people, while the Calormenes use it more as a sweetened flavor.

The table was bare when they entered, but it was of course a magic table, and at a word from the old man the tablecloth, silver plates, glasses, and food appeared.
—THE VOYAGE OF THE DAWN TREADER

5 CUPS SYRUP

3 lemons
4 cups water
2½ cups granulated sugar
1 teaspoon citric acid, available from specialty stores

TO SERVE:

Water, sparkling or uncarbonated
Lemon slices
Sprigs of mint

1. Cut the whole lemons into quarters, remove the seeds, and puree in the blender with 1 cup of water.

2. Put the lemon pulp into a saucepan with the remaining water, the sugar, and citric acid, and bring to a boil, stirring until the sugar is dissolved.

3. Remove from heat. Cool. Strain into a clean bottle, cap, and store in the refrigerator.

4. To serve, place ice in a tall glass. Add 2 parts water to 1 part lemon base, or to taste. Garnish with slices of lemon and mint sprigs if desired.

104

SHERBET

The origin of sherbet can be traced back to the dawn of the Arab nations of the world, where it was developed as a soothing, fruit-flavored fizzy drink. Arab people do not believe in alcoholic drinks and prepared sherbets as an invigorating substitute. They are also especially good in the very hot and dry environments of the desert, where people get extremely thirsty. Calormenes drink wine as well as sherbets, but sherbet is a better thirst quencher than any wine.

He had never even imagined lying on anything so comfortable as that sofa or drinking anything so delicious as that sherbet.
—THE HORSE AND HIS BOY

Pineapple Sherbet

1. Place ⅓ of the pineapple chunks into the jar of a blender with ⅓ of the lemon juice and ⅓ of the pineapple juice. Blend until the mixture is as smooth as possible. Transfer into a covered container.

2. Repeat with the remaining fruit and juice, in two more batches.

3. Taste and add honey or sugar to desired sweetness. Refrigerate.

4. To serve, place some ice in a tall glass. Shake the sherbet well and pour over the ice. Garnish with a sprig of mint.

6–8 SERVINGS

1 fresh pineapple, as sweet and ripe as possible, peeled, cored, and cut into chunks, about 4½ cups
Juice of 3 lemons, about 9 tablespoons
4 cups canned pineapple juice
Honey or sugar to taste
Sprigs of fresh mint

One pint of fresh straw-
  berries, hulled and
  washed, about 4 cups
2 cups water
Juice of 2 lemons, about 6
  tablespoons
Honey or sugar to taste

Strawberry Sherbet

1. Place ⅓ of the strawberries into the jar of a blender with ⅓ of the lemon juice and ⅓ of the water. Blend until the mixture is as smooth as possible. Transfer into a covered container.

2. Repeat with the remaining fruit, juice, and water, in two more batches.

3. Taste and add honey or sugar to desired sweetness. Refrigerate.

4. To serve, place some ice in a tall glass. Shake the sherbet well and pour over the ice.

♦

COFFEE AND HOT MILK

Coffee beans are not really beans at all. They are berries, bright red when they are ripe, that are fermented in the sun for a few days and then gradually dried for about three weeks. After drying, the berries are milled to separate the berry husk from the seed inside, and that seed is what is known to us as the coffee bean. Coffee beans are roasted to give them the delicious aroma and flavor with which we are so familiar. Calormen has the hot sun needed for drying berries, and the hills south of Tashbaan are a suitable area for growing coffee.

By the time Shasta had finished his porridge, the Dwarf's two brothers (whose names were Rogin and Bricklethumb) were putting the dish of bacon and eggs and mushrooms, and the coffeepot and the hot milk, and the toast, on the table.

—*THE HORSE AND HIS BOY*

Use your favorite method for making coffee. The drip method produces a particularly pleasing result.

To drip coffee:

1. Preheat the pot with boiling water.

2. Place a gold or paper filter in the holder and scoop in measured drip grind coffee. Place on top of the heated pot.

3. Pour the proper amount of boiling water over the grounds and allow to drip through into pot. Remove the filter top and serve the coffee.

Coffee may be transferred to an insulated jug to keep hot. Never reheat or boil coffee.

To serve:

Heat milk to scalding but do not boil. Pour equal

PER CUP:

2 tablespoons freshly ground coffee, your own favorite roast
8 ounces (½ cup) fresh cold water
Sugar and milk or cream to taste

amounts of milk and coffee into a coffee cup or mug and add sugar to taste. Cream may be used in place of milk. Whip the cream to very soft peaks and float on top of the coffee after the beverage is sweetened. A sprinkling of cinnamon or grated chocolate can be added for flavor.

Coffee Calormene

1. Using a Turkish coffeepot or a small saucepan, bring the water and the sugar to a hard boil. Remove the pot from the heat and stir in the coffee.

2. Return the pot to the heat. The coffee will boil up quickly. Remove it from the heat for a few seconds until the boiling subsides. Return the pot to the heat, bring to a boil for a second time, and remove from heat again for a few seconds. When the coffee simmers down, return to the heat for a third time. Allow it to come to a final boil and before the grounds settle, pour the coffee into Turkish coffee cups or espresso cups, spooning a teaspoonful of foam into each cup.

Note: The grounds of Turkish coffee are a fine powder and settle to the bottom of each cup. They may be sipped with the coffee or not as you please.

6 SMALL CUPS

2 cups boiling water
1–6 teaspoons granulated
  sugar, depending upon
  desired sweetness
2 tablespoons Turkish
  coffee

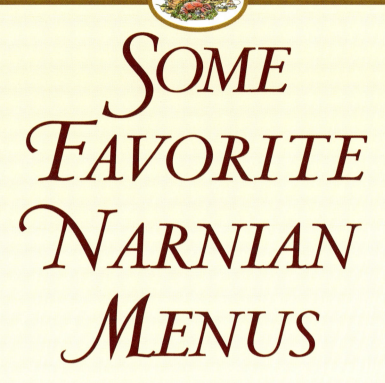

SOME FAVORITE NARNIAN MENUS

SOME FAVORITE NARNIAN MENUS

Breakfast

BREAKFAST AT CASTLE ANVARD (WINTER)

Porridge
Scrambled eggs and toast
Pot of tea

♦

BREAKFAST WITH THE DWARFS

Bacon, eggs, mushrooms, and sausages
Everyday white bread
Pot of strong tea

♦

TELMARINE BREAKFAST

Stewed figs
English omelette
Everyday white bread
Pot of coffee

Lunch

ARCHENLAND PICNIC

Pigeon pie
Cold ham (served with assorted luncheon salads)
Mead or sherbet
Tea cakes with lemon curd filling

♦

LUNCH AT CAIR PARAVEL

Main Course:
Cold lamb and green peas (served with potato salad)
Dessert:
Gooseberry fool
A selection of fresh fruits
Drinks:
Lemon squash
Sherbet
Coffee

♦

NARNIAN WAYFARER'S LUNCH

Meat pasty
Apples, herbs, and cheese
Mead

Afternoon Tea

TEA WITH MR. TUMNUS

Boiled egg and Scotch eggs
Sardines on toast
Oatcakes
Sugar-topped cake
A lovely cup of hot tea

Dinner

State Banquet at Cair Paravel

Appetizer:
Mushroom soup
Lobster salad
Main Course:
Boiled and glazed ham
Roast pheasant (served
  with roast potatoes and
  a wide variety of
  vegetables)
Dessert:
Steamed pudding with hot
  chocolate sauce
Strawberry Ice Cream
Fresh fruit
Drinks:
Mead, lemon squash,
  sherbet (grown-ups could
  drink a white wine with
  the fish course, a light
  red or rosé with the
  ham, and a sharp dessert
  wine, Château Coutet de
  Barsac perhaps, with the
  dessert)

◆

Dinner with Good Giants (suitable for powerful appetites)

Soup:
Cock-a-leekie soup
Appetizer:
Cold poached salmon
Homestyle brown bread

Main Course:
Traditional roast turkey
Grilled loin of venison
Boiled potatoes
Wide variety of vegetables
Salad:
Green salad with salad
  cream dressing (or
  Gresham Dressing)
Dessert:
Marmalade roll
Ginger fig pudding
Mincemeat pies
(all served with vanilla cus-
  tard sauce)
Finisher:
Turkish delight
Sweetmeats
Toffee
Hot chocolate

◆

Supper with Puddleglum: A Marsh-wiggle Meal

Appetizer:
Sardines on toast
Main Course:
Fresh fried fish (pavenders
  for preference; trout will
  do)
Stewed eel
Boiled potatoes
Salad greens

Dessert:
Mixed fruit jelly with
  cream
Fresh fruit
Drinks:
Coffee or tea

◆

The Tisroc's Feast of Tash

Appetizer:
Chicken breast masquerad-
  ing as snipe
Chicken livers Calormene
Dried figs
Main Course:
Roast pheasant
Grilled loin of venison
Roast lamb
Sausage
Boiled rice
Dessert:
Strawberry ice
Fresh fruit
Tea cakes with lemon curd
  filling
Orange jelly
Drinks:
Lemon squash
Sherbet
Finisher:
Turkish delight
Coffee Calormene

INDEX